VIVA
Bloom's
NOTES

William Golding's
LORD OF THE FLIES

Edited and with an Introduction by
HAROLD BLOOM

Viva Books
New Delhi | Mumbai | Chennai | Kolkata | Bangalore | Hyderabad | Kochi | Guwahati

First Indian Edition 2007
Reprinted 2010

VIVA BOOKS PRIVATE LIMITED

- 4737/23 Ansari Road, Daryaganj, New Delhi 110 002
  E-mail: vivadelhi@vivagroupindia.net, Tel. 42242200
- 76, Service Industries, Shirvane, Sector 1, Nerul, Navi Mumbai 400 706
  E-mail: vivamumbai@vivagroupindia.net, Tel. 27721273, 27721274
- Jamals Fazal Chambers, 26 Greams Road, Chennai 600 006
  E-mail: vivachennai@vivagroupindia.net, Tel. 28290304, 28294241
- B-103, Jindal Towers, 21/1A/3 Darga Road, Kolkata 700 017
  E-mail: vivakolkata@vivagroupindia.net, Tel. 22836381, 22816713
- 7, Sovereign Park Apartments, 56-58, K. R. Road, Basavanagudi, Bangalore 560 004
  E-mail: vivabangalore@vivagroupindia.net, Tel. 26607409, 26607410
- 101-102 Mughal Marc Apartments, 3-4-637 to 641, Narayanguda, Hyderabad 500 029
  E-mail: vivahyderabad@vivagroupindia.net, Tel. 27564481, 27564482
- First Floor, Beevi Towers, SRM Road, Kaloor, Kochi 682 018, Kerala
  E-mail: vivakochi@vivagroupindia.net, Tel: 0484-2403055, 2403056
- 232, GNB Road, Beside UCO Bank, Silpukhuri, Guwahati 781 003
  E-mail: vivaguwahati@vivagroupindia.net, Tel: 0361-2666386

www.vivagroupindia.com

Published by arrangement with

Facts on File, Inc.
132 West 31st Street
New York 10001
USA

ISBN 978-81-309-0452-8

All links and web addresses were checked and verified to be correct at the time of publications. Because of the dynamic nature of the web, some addresses and links may have changed since publication and may no longer be valid.

Every effort has been made to trace the owners of copyrighted materialand secure copyright permission. Articles appearing in this volume generally appear much as they did in their original publication with little to no editorial changes. Those interested in locating the original source will find bibliographic information on the first page of each article as well as in the bibliography and acknowledgments sections of this volume.

Published by Vinod Vasishtha for Viva Books Private Limited, 4737/23, Ansari Road, Daryaganj, New Delhi-110 002. Printed and bound by Anand Sons, Delhi - 110092.

Contents

User's Guide

This volume is designed to present biographical, critical, and bibliographical information on William Golding and *Lord of the Flies*. Following Harold Bloom's introduction, there appears a detailed biography of the author, discussing the major events in his life and his important literary works. Then follows a thematic and structural analysis of the work, in which significant themes, patterns, and motifs are traced. An annotated list of characters supplies brief information on the chief characters in the work.

A selection of critical extracts, derived from previously published material by leading critics, then follows. The extracts consist of statements by the author on his work, early reviews of the work, and later evaluations down to the present day. The items are arranged chronologically by date of first publication. A bibliography of Golding's writings (including a complete listing of all books he wrote, cowrote, edited, and translated, and selected posthumous publications), a list of additional books and articles on him and on *Lord of the Flies*, and an index of themes and ideas conclude the volume.

Harold Bloom is Sterling Professor of the Humanities at Yale University and Henry W. and Albert A. Berg Professor of English at the New York University Graduate School. He is the author of twenty books and the editor of more than thirty anthologies of literature and literary criticism.

Professor Bloom's works include *Shelley's Mythmaking* (1959), *The Visionary Company* (1961), *Blake's Apocalypse* (1963), *Yeats* (1970), *A Map of Misreading* (1975), *Kabbalah and Criticism* (1975), and *Agon: Towards a Theory of Revisionism* (1982). *The Anxiety of Influence* (1973) sets forth Professor Bloom's provocative theory of the literary relationships between the great writers and their predecessors. His most recent books are *The American Religion* (1992) and *The Western Canon* (1994).

Professor Bloom earned his Ph.D. from Yale University in 1955 and has served on the Yale faculty since then. He is a 1985 MacArthur Foundation Award recipient and served as the Charles Eliot Norton Professor of Poetry at Harvard University in 1987–88. He is currently the editor of the Chelsea House series Major Literary Characters and Modern Critical Views, and other Chelsea House series in literary criticism.

Introduction

HAROLD BLOOM

The survival of *Lord of the Flies* (1954), half a century after its initial publication, is not in itself a testimony to the book's permanence, even as a popular fiction of the boy's adventure story genre. Golding, a schoolmaster for many years, clearly knew a good deal about the psychology of young boys, particularly in regard to group dynamics. Whether the psychological representations of *Lord of the Flies* remain altogether convincing seems to me rather questionable; the saintly Simon strains credibility as a naturalistic portrait. In many ways the book is remarkably tendentious, and too clearly has a program to urge upon us. Overt moral allegory, even in a lively adventure story, may arouse our resentments, and I find it difficult to reread *Lord of the Flies* without a certain skepticism towards Golding's designs upon his reader. In some sense, the book is Mark Twain turned upside down, and I mean the Mark Twain of *Roughing It* rather than of *Adventures of Huckleberry Finn.* Sometimes I like to try the critical experiment of pretending to be Mark Twain as I read *Lord of the Flies:* How *would* Huck Finn have reacted to the regressive saga of the English schoolboys of *Lord of the Flies?* We cannot find any trace of Huck in Ralph or in Jack, in Simon or in Piggy or in Roger. Golding, I think, would have been furious at my suggestion that this has something to do with Huck's being American, and Golding's boys being British. Original Sin is not a very American idea, and the wonderful skepticism of Huck, at any age, would have preserved him from being either an implausible saint or a bestial hunter. This is hardly to suggest that we are less savage or violence-prone than the British; Huck knows better, and we know better. But it may indicate some of the limitations of *Lord of the Flies;* as a grim fable, unrelieved in its rigor, it lacks all humor, and is an involuntary parody of Twain's *Roughing It* or his *Innocents Abroad.*

Golding once said that the dead parachutist in *Lord of the Flies* was meant to represent "History," in the adult sense. The moral implication that Golding intended doubtless was that the group reversion to organized savagery in his book was no different from adult reversion, at any time. Whether a reader finds this convincing seems to me quite disputable: an American might want to reply, with Ralph Waldo Emerson, that there is no history, only biography. Golding's fable is vivid and is narrated with great skill, but is it a fable of universal relevance? At the end, Golding tells us that "Ralph wept for the end of innocence, the darkness of man's heart." Are we moved by Ralph's weeping, or do we flinch at it because of Golding's inverted sentimentalism? Emotion in excess of the object that provokes it tends to be a pragmatic definition of sentimentality. I suspect that it comes down to the issue of universalism: do the boys of *Lord of the Flies* represent the human condition, or do they reflect the traditions of British schools with their restrictive structures, sometimes brutal discipline, and not always benign visions of human nature? Golding himself said that society, whether in life or in *Lord of the Flies,* plays only a minor role in bringing about human violence and depravity. But what about the one society his boys truly have known, the society of their schools? One can admire *Lord of the Flies* as a tale of adventure, while wondering whether its moral fable was not far more insular than Golding seems to have realized. ✤

Biography of William Golding

William Gerald Golding was born on September 19, 1911, in St. Columb Minor, Cornwall, the son of Alec Golding, a noted schoolteacher, and Mildred A. Golding. William led a somewhat isolated childhood, spent largely in the company of his nurse, Lily. He was a prodigious reader as a boy, and at the age of twelve he conceived the idea of writing a twelve-volume novel cycle on the trade union movement; but he wrote only a few pages. He attended Marlborough Grammar School and then Brasenose College, Oxford. He first thought of securing a degree in science, but after two years he switched to English, becoming immersed in Anglo-Saxon literature—an outgrowth of his lifelong fascination with primitive cultures. Golding graduated in 1935. While at Oxford, he published *Poems* (1934), a volume he later repudiated.

Golding became a social worker at a London settlement house; during his spare time he wrote, produced, and acted with small theatre companies. He married Ann Brookfield in 1939; they had a son and a daughter. Golding began teaching at Bishop Wordsworth's School in Salisbury shortly before World War II but entered the Royal Navy in 1940. He served for five years, achieving the rank of lieutenant and being stationed mostly on various vessels in the North Atlantic; in 1944 he participated in the D day invasion of Normandy. The war was perhaps the defining moment in Golding's life, and much of the rest of his work draws either directly or metaphorically upon his war experiences.

Golding returned to Bishop Wordsworth's School in 1945, where he taught for another sixteen years. In 1960 he received an M.A. from Brasenose College. During 1961–62 he was writer-in-residence at Hollins College; for the rest of his life he was a full-time writer.

After the war Golding wrote three novels, but they were not published. Then, in 1954, he issued *Lord of the Flies,* (1954), a gripping parable in which a group of English schoolboys stranded on an island descend into savagery. It was rejected by twenty-one publishers before finally being accepted. The initial reviews were mixed, and sales were steady but not remarkable; but in the late 1950s, as a result of praise from American intellectuals, the novel developed enormous popularity in the United States and has become one of the most widely read works in high schools, surpassing even J. D. Salinger's *The Catcher in the Rye* for a time. A film adaptation was released in 1963; a remake appeared in 1990.

Golding's next novel, *The Inheritors* (1955), was another tale of savagery, this time that of the Homo sapiens who drive the Neanderthals to extinction. Many critics believe it to be superior to its predecessor. Shortly after its publication Golding was named a Fellow of the Royal Society of Literature. *Pincher Martin* (1956) is a strikingly allusive and elliptical novel about a wounded soldier during World War II who tries to survive on a barren island in the North Atlantic; it bears some thematic relationship to *Lord of the Flies*. *Free Fall* (1959) is the story of a painter who enlists in the army and is made a prisoner of war by the Nazis. Golding's novels of the 1950s established him as one of the leading voices in British fiction, and his critical recognition seemed assured.

In the 1960s, however, Golding became strangely silent, issuing only one novel, *The Spire* (1964), a tale of art and religion set in the fourteenth century, a very poorly received collection of novellas, *The Pyramid* (1967), and a volume of essays, *The Hot Gates and Other Occasional Pieces* (1965). After another volume of novellas, *The Scorpion God: Three Short Novels* (1971) (one of which, "Envoy Extraordinary," was a work written years before and was adapted into the play *The Brass Butterfly*, 1958), no new work by Golding was published for eight years.

Critics who had counted him out were pleasantly surprised when Golding began again to produce novels on a par with his earliest: *Darkness Visible* (1979), about a crazed Pentecostal prophet; *Rites of Passage* (1980), set in the early nineteenth century on board a ship that is taking a colonial governor to Australia; *The Paper Men* (1984), a bitter work about a novelist and his biographer; and *Close Quarters* (1987) and *Fire Down*

Below (1989), which comprise a trilogy with *Rites of Passage.* Golding also issued a collection of essays and lectures, *A Moving Target* (1982), as well as a travel volume, *An Egyptian Journal* (1985).

Golding was made a CBE (Commander of the British Empire) and an honorary fellow of Brasenose College in 1966, won the Nobel Prize for literature in 1983, and was knighted in 1988. He died in Perranarworthal, England, on June 19, 1993. A draft of a novel, *The Double Tongue,* was published in 1995. ♣

Thematic and Structural Analysis

Lord of the Flies opens on a tropical island. Ralph, a boy of about twelve, wanders aimlessly among the thick vegetation. Another schoolboy is in quick pursuit; quite plump and wearing glasses, he appears glad to find someone else. They acknowledge each other, but Ralph is clearly not interested in bonding. The chubby boy's accent is not as polished as Ralph's. He announces to Ralph that he suffers from asthma, "ass-mar" as he calls it. Ralph mocks the accent and continues on his walk while the other boy tries to make polite introductions. Instead of giving his Christian name, he asks Ralph not to call him what the other boys at school did, that is, Piggy. This name provokes Ralph to great laughter and instantly becomes Piggy's permanent label. Piggy's physical condition may discourage Ralph's interest, but the isolation of the island soon fosters an early but unacknowledged relationship between them. As they walk, Piggy finds a conch on the beach and relates to Ralph how it can be used like a trumpet. After a couple of tries, Ralph successfully sounds the conch. As a result, boys begin to appear from all points of the island. Ralph and Piggy are joined by about twenty-five boys in school uniform. There is general conversation among them as they sit on a platform in the sand. Then, along the beach, they see a group of boys dressed in choir garb. Their heavy clothing stands out because of the intense heat of the island. They march and sing as they approach the group. They are led by Jack, the lead choirboy.

Thus, in **chapter one**, all the players in Golding's simple yet brutal tale are now present. There is not much explanation given by Golding about how the boys have arrived on this island. A plane, a pilot, and an atom bomb are mentioned in passing. No adult seems to have survived the apparent airplane accident that brought the boys here. Nor do they appear to know each other well, with the exception of the choirboys. They know, or rather recognize, each other as fellow schoolboys, that is, public schoolboys, and consequently members of the British elite.

Instinctively, the boys respond to the authoritative trappings of their society at the outset. The conch, whose loud noise summons the boys together, is the first totem of civilization. Then, in a haphazard way, the boys use another of society's conventions: they put the leadership of the group to a vote. This provokes the first of the many struggles between Ralph and Jack. Ralph is chosen leader, somewhat by default because of the conch, even though Jack had considered himself the only logical choice. To appease Jack, Ralph reminds him that he is still in charge of the choirboys. Ralph suggests that they might serve as an army, but Jack instead prefers the idea of their being hunters. With this settled, Ralph turns the attention of the group to the essential tasks at hand. They must scan the terrain and determine whether they are indeed on an island. Ralph and Jack, joined by Simon, start off when Piggy insists on following. Ralph wants nothing to do with him and is successful in diverting Piggy's interests only by giving him the task of taking names. This appeals to Piggy, who sets out to take inventory of the group.

On their search, the three boys get some idea of the island's shape and size. Their trek is marked by three milestones. First, while making the somewhat arduous climb, they come upon piles of large sharp rocks. One is loose enough to move, so together they sway it back and forth until it falls into the forest below. "Like a bomb," one of the boys remarks, as they all savor their triumph over the stone and their new world. Next, as they climb to the highest point, they confirm the fact that they are on an island. From this vantage point, they can see not only the platform near the lagoon where they left the other boys but also the place where they landed, marked by a gash in the trees. Ralph's shouts of "This belongs to us" and "All ours" are countered by Jack's insistence on finding food. As they start the descent, the third milestone occurs when, in the thick of the forest, they come across a squealing piglet caught in a thicket. Jack pulls out a knife and raises it for the kill. But a moment of hesitation on Jack's part allows the piglet enough time to escape. All three boys are caught up in the terror of what might have happened. Their nervous laughter breaks the tension for only a moment. Jack vows to show no mercy the next time.

In **chapter two**, Ralph calls the group together to report the findings of their search. Since they are on an island and there are no "grownups" around, they must fend for themselves. Jack interrupts to relate the tale of the piglet. Ralph tries to keep order by agreeing that Jack's hunters can search for food and meat. Because of the general excitement and disorder, Ralph announces that whoever holds the conch can talk and all must listen quietly. Jack agrees with the idea of having lots of rules. Almost unseen, Piggy removes the conch from Ralph's lap, and all become quiet. Piggy emphasizes that nobody knows of the boys' whereabouts. Ralph responds to the logic of Piggy's observations. He takes back the conch to give support to Piggy's remarks and to reassure the assembly that their situation is not hopeless.

The ritual holding of the conch is quickly established. It is used to anchor the two primary episodes of the chapter. First, a small boy with a wine-colored scar on his face holds out his hands to get the conch. He comes from among the "littluns," the little boys of the group who tend to stay together. Even though the boy holds the conch, he is overwhelmed by the laughter of the older boys. He cannot speak himself, and so he whispers to Piggy, who acts as his interpreter for the group. The small boy reports the sighting of a snake-thing, a "Beastie." Despite the attempts by the older boys to laugh it off as the product of a nightmare, the image of the Beast introduces fear into the group.

Ralph takes over the conch and tries to refocus the attention of the group. He denies the existence of any snake-thing. He sets out two goals: to have fun and to get rescued. As he thinks out loud, he refers to two images of comfort and support: his father in the navy, and the queen. This begins to distract the group from the squeamish subject of the Beast. Then Ralph introduces the heart of the second episode of the chapter: He states that to be discovered they must make a smoke fire. Thus, the fire not only removes the specter of fear but gives the boys a concrete method of meeting the goals Ralph has set. They all begin the climb to the top of the mountain, where they collect as much wood as possible.

The challenge of lighting the fire introduces yet another totem of power in Golding's tale. In the absence of matches,

Piggy's "specs" are grabbed from his face by Jack to start the first fire. But the rotten wood and the poor design of this first attempt soon turn the mountaintop into a fiery failure. Piggy brings the group unwillingly back to reason, but Jack will have none of him or his logic. He responds only to Ralph, who suggests that more rules are needed, especially regarding the maintenance of the fire. Jack agrees and makes his hunters responsible for keeping up the fire. He adds, "After all, we're not savages. We're English, and the English are best at everything." Piggy, though, sees through the bravura to the dark side of their situation. The smoldering first fire catches on to creepers and sparks carry it through leaves and brush until it spreads down to consume part of the nearby forest. At the sight, the boys break into a cheer. Piggy, still holding the conch, demands their attention. Because of his annoying regard for reason, it appears impossible for Piggy to bring the crowd to order. He chastises them for acting like kids. Ralph and Jack, both in their own way, are unsuccessful in dissuading Piggy from his speech. The episode ends as night falls and fear returns as Piggy brings to the attention of all the unexplained disappearance of the boy with the wine-colored scar.

Chapter three provides a closer look at Ralph, Jack, and Simon. The chapter opens with Jack attempting his first hunt. He has armed himself with a spear and is able to track down a pig but fails at the moment of attack. He returns to find Ralph, who is involved in the complicated task of constructing shelters. Ralph complains that only Simon has stayed behind to help. Both Jack's hunters and the other boys, according to Ralph, have been involved in less essential activities. Ralph and Jack continue to struggle with their relationship, their roles in the group, and with the ever-returning fear of the unmentionable Beast. Next, Golding's narration switches to a profile of Simon. After he abandons Jack and Ralph to explore the forest, he comes upon an overgrowth of vegetation. As the chapter ends, he crawls furtively into its center to discover a cabinlike space, sealed off from view by the cover of leaves and filled with the sensuality of nature.

In the beginning of **chapter four**, some rhythm of life has settled in for the boys. This is marked by the sun's stages throughout the day. Golding's narration diverts somewhat from the dialogue in the previous chapters to a descriptive differentiation of the boys. The younger boys are about six years old. Their activities include eating too much fruit, sleeping when they please, and playing on the beach. Henry, Johnny, and Percival are exemplary littluns. These three in particular have been engaged in making sand castles on the beach when Maurice and Roger, two of the bigger boys, return from tending the fire. The difference of age, category, and, consequently, power is felt and acknowledged immediately.

The older boys' activities threaten the carefully made castles of the younger ones. Roger even begins a stone-throwing, slow-motion intimidation of young Henry's space, but only up to a certain point, since the rules of their old life still govern both their unconscious and conscious actions. Golding's very silent yet palpable narration is felt more heavily here in a small detail: "Roger's arm was conditioned by a civilization that knew nothing of him and was in ruins." This detail, like that of the plane crash (as well as the reason for the plane trip), receives mention yet is left without explanation. But this very slight opening to a historical thread is closed by Jack's summoning the two older boys to witness his pig hunting. The change of focus is hardly gratuitous. With Jack's insistence on the hunt, a chain of events begins what will be the downward spiral of the boys' very precariously defined new world.

While Jack is busy fabricating camouflage makeup, Ralph, Piggy, and Simon, along with some of the others, are enjoying some time after a dip in their bathing pool. The disheveled state of their clothes illustrates the passage of time on the island. What should have been a quiet rest is abruptly interrupted by Ralph's sighting of a ship. Excitement is quickly replaced by panic when Ralph realizes that their signal fire is out. He runs to get Piggy's glasses to light a new fire only to realize that it is too late. In the middle of Ralph's furious reaction to their plight, Jack returns and euphorically announces his success in killing a pig. Exhilaration faces common sense as the two boys stare at each other. Jack refuses to let the confrontation diminish his triumph. He rashly grabs off the glasses from Piggy's face, not in anticipation of lighting a cooking fire but thinking first of wounding Piggy and Ralph in turn. Ralph chides him for the dirty trick. Jack is forced to apologize publicly and loses face once again to Ralph. Jack and his hunters now set about to build the cooking fire, but Jack must depend on Ralph's intervention. Without Piggy's glasses, Jack cannot light the fire to roast his prize pig. Ralph borrows the glasses for this purpose, and reinforces, for the present, his position as leader. In the excitement of cooking and then eating, the group recounts the exploits of the hunt. The frenzy of their cries is only interrupted by Ralph's announcing assembly, conch in hand.

Chapter five opens with Ralph confronting the ever-worsening situation at hand. He has called assembly, he says, not to laugh or roll off the log but to set things straight. On one level Ralph's agenda is nonthreatening for the boys. He reminds them of rules of hygiene (which causes general tittering among the crowd) and the need for shelter. He steps on delicate ground, though, when he tries to make the point that maintaining the fire is more important than hunting pigs. Jack reacts, as is now expected. Thus the tokens of fire and hunting represent the struggle for power between the two boys. The conch, as it is passed or grabbed, is challenged for its role as power symbol, as is Ralph's role as leader.

Ralph then brings up an agenda item that upsets them all—the existence of fear, the Beast, things in the night. Young Phil is allowed to recount a nightmare, then Percival cannot recite, as is his habit, his complete name and address. Both actions undermine any little remaining control the boys have over the dark side of their fear; the littluns start to cry. Jack in his usual abrupt way breaks the tension with shouts of bravado. Ralph warns the boys that things are "slipping away," that is, civilization and order are giving way to nightmares and dark fantasies. Jack challenges this remark and, in turn, Ralph as leader. The boy who once wanted rules now claims that they are not necessary. Jack and his gang run off, leaving Simon, Piggy, and Ralph in the dark. Despite Piggy's persistent dependence on common sense, as night falls the three are plunged into heavy thought, interrupted only by Percival's wailing.

The boys are surrounded by the darkness of night at the beginning of **chapter six**. Despite their fears, they finally fall asleep. It is a moonlit night and the explosion in the sky that takes place is quite visible, though none of the boys are awake to notice it or the parachutist dropping from the sky. The winds come and go and drag the dangling, seemingly lifeless body of the parachutist over the island. The body lands in a tangle of lines, which are caught up in the rocks. Its only movement is caused by the wind that tightens or slackens the lines. In the meantime, it is Samneric's turn to tend the fire. Samneric is a name the boys have given to a pair of twins, Sam and Eric, who are so psychologically close that they seem to function as one being. They have both fallen asleep, since neither is able to stay awake on his own. They both wake and in the silence of the morning hear the movement of the parachute fabric. Startled at the sight in the distance, they run off to awaken Ralph. Assembly is called and Samneric report their sighting of the Beast. Their grotesque description awakens fear in the boys. Jack immediately calls for a hunt. Ralph breaks off yet another crisis by reminding them of the need to tend the fire. As the boys calm down, Ralph sets out a plan to search the island for the beast. They head for the remote end of the island where not even Jack has explored. It is rough and dangerous terrain. At a particularly treacherous passage, Ralph, as leader, offers to go ahead on his own; Jack catches up later. They find no beast, but Jack is excited by the wildness of the area. They report back to the waiting boys, who seem duly relieved by the news and attracted, as Jack is, to the possibilities of a new area to explore. The enthusiasm for creating a fort and rolling rocks off the cliffs engages them more than searching for, and consequently acknowledging, any beast. Jack wins out as Ralph's control of the group begins its rapid decline.

At the start of **chapter seven**, Ralph decides to acquiesce to Jack's wishes as long as this allows the group to forget the Beast for awhile. Then, on a break from play to eat fruit, Ralph privately takes stock of his physical condition and realizes the new conditions—dirty clothes, no bath, no toothbrush—he now takes as normal ones. Simon picks up on Ralph's reverie and reassures him that they will be rescued. On their way back across the island, Simon volunteers to go ahead alone to tell Piggy that the others are continuing on in their search. The group heads for the pig-run in the forest, since it leads up to the mountain. At the end of the pig-run, Ralph decides to postpone the climb for the light of day. Jack challenges Ralph, who reluctantly accepts the long climb up the mountainside. They both take Roger along on what becomes an arduous climb in the dark. At the top, Jack goes ahead and sights something. Ralph continues on, and as they all come together, they spot the shape of a beast, apparently with its head in its knees. The wind blows, and the beast lifts its head. The boys, taken by fear, run off into the darkness below.

In **chapter eight**, the news of the Beast's sighting provokes yet another, more profound, confrontation between Jack and Ralph. At assembly, Jack accuses Ralph of cowardice and declares, "He says things like Piggy. He isn't a proper chief." Red in the face, Jack takes this tactic one step too far and calls for a vote against Ralph's leadership. He is met with deadly silence. The sting of this betrayal by the group brings tears to his eyes. As he storms off, Ralph tries to call him back but Jack will have nothing of him. He walks off in tears, but not before issuing a mutinous invitation to any who wish to follow him.

Piggy's voice of reason breaks the extreme tension of the moment. The fire remains their priority, and since the Beast is too close to the one on the mountain, Piggy suggests that they build a fire on the beach. The wood there is not as easy to gather, but the task occupies all. At the sight of the fire, the littluns start to dance and sing around it. While resting, Ralph begins to notice how few of the older boys are present. Piggy confirms this and relates seeing them leave gradually while the others were gathering wood. Simon, too, is nowhere to be found. He has not joined Jack as the others did; instead, he has retreated to his hiding place deep in the forest. On the other side of the island, Jack takes stock of his group. The choirboys who were once joined in song now focus their attention on Jack's words. He states that they will forget the Beast and dream less on this part of the island. They will occupy themselves as hunters should. Bolstered by these words, they enter the forest and begin what becomes a brutal hunt and slaughter of a sow. The violence of the kill and its sexual overtones thrill the boys. They cover themselves in the sow's blood and reenact the violent scene. Then Jack declares that the group will rob fire from the others so they can roast the pig. But before this, they sever the sow's head. Roger has sharpened a stick at both ends, at Jack's urging. The boys plunge the stick in the earth and impale the head on the other end. Jack declares that the head is their gift to the Beast. The boys run off, not knowing that Simon in his hideaway has witnessed the fateful offering. Caught up in the isolation of the space, Simon becomes consumed by the sight of the pig's head.

Back at the fire, Ralph worries about their fate. Piggy assures him and the others that the fire continues to be their most important goal. Out of the forest, screaming hunters rush into the space, producing fear in the littluns. Some hunters run off with half-burnt branches; three, in war paint, remain. One of these is Jack, who has been emboldened by his triumphs and now invites all to join him in their upcoming feast and fun. Once again, though, Piggy reminds the remaining boys that they must tend the fire. This scene shifts rapidly to Simon and the pig's head. The Beast, acknowledged by the boys' offering, now takes on the identity of the Lord of the Flies. It speaks to Simon and taunts him. Struck silent by a paralyzing fear, Simon falls down in a faint.

As **chapter nine** begins, Simon makes a vital discovery. His faint, and later sleep, have left him weak but eager to get out of the forest. He climbs up and ends up on the mountaintop. He spots the Beast and slowly approaches it. He discovers the reality of the dead parachutist and the mechanics of its movements. Simon untangles the lines of the chute, freeing the body. Simon gets a good look at death and is sick at the sight of it, but then quickly comprehends the need to communicate the news to the rest.

Meanwhile, Jack and his band of hunters are reveling in their feast. Piggy and Ralph watch from a distance. Jack offers them meat and encourages all present to join his tribe. Jack takes advantage of the crowd to continue his taunting of Ralph. All the while, the weather is changing radically. Piggy suggests that they leave to avoid further confrontation between Jack and Ralph. Jack encourages the madness of the hunters, who begin another reenactment of the hunt. Thunder undermines the nerve of all present and the littluns scatter. The hunters' hysteria continues to intensify at Jack's urging. The thunder, as much as the fearful screams of the littluns, seems to provoke them to further frenzy. They repeat over and over their hunting chant,

"Kill the beast! Cut his throat! Spill his blood!" Their frenzy is so great that they do not recognize the thing crawling out of the forest. They circle it and throw their spears. The hunted shape struggles and reaches the edge of a rock. It falls wounded to the sand below. The crowd leaps down after it and attacks it with greater fury. Just then the clouds open with a heavy rain, dispersing the young hunters. The blood of their kill stains the sand. On the mountaintop, the forceful wind of the storm takes the body of the parachutist and deposits it in the sea. Around midnight, the tempest ends, leaving clear skies and cool air. The dead "beast" lies quietly on the beach. The tide pulls the body of Simon, and the water quietly carries it out to sea.

As **chapter ten** opens, Piggy and Ralph cannot ignore their brutal reality. They try to put a name to the events of the previous night; was it murder or an accident? But like the Beast before, Simon's fate is not labeled, as if this lack of definition will remove the specter of his death from the boys' thoughts. In the meantime, the remote section of the island, Castle Rock, has been transformed into the hunters' fort. Sentries have been placed at the entrance. Jack rules as chief inside the cave, from where he sets out the rules and deals out the punishments for any violations. The subject of the previous night's gruesome episode is brought up indirectly. Like Piggy and Ralph, Jack avoids any definitive description of the events. He will say only that the Beast came disguised and thus dismisses the subject. He promises confidently to all that they will hunt again.

On the other side of the island, Ralph, Piggy, Samneric, and some littluns are the only ones who have not joined Jack's tribe. As before, Ralph is contemplating their state and their dismal prospects for maintaining the fire, and consequently for rescue. Some calm comes over them for a time until, in a sudden attack, Jack and two of his cronies lay siege on them. Ralph struggles as best he can, but to no avail. Afterward, he and the twins pick Piggy out of the wreckage of one of the shelters. Piggy, still holding on to his belief in order, thought that the attack was to capture the conch, and thus the symbol of authority. Instead, Jack and his men have taken Piggy's specs. They walk along the beach, heading back to Castle Rock. Jack's trot displays his exultation. He has triumphed and is now the undisputed leader. He has Piggy's specs, the totem of true power, in his hands.

In **chapter eleven**, there are only four boys left and these few realize their predicament. All others have joined Jack's tribe at Castle Rock. Ralph tries to restart the fire, but sees that his efforts are useless. Without Piggy's glasses, they will be unable to have a fire. The consequences of this fact are too heavy to consider. The four decide that the only thing left to do is to confront Jack on his own turf and demand the return of Piggy's glasses to restart the signal fire. As they approach Castle Rock, they are met by one of Jack's sentries. Ralph stands his ground and announces that he is there to call assembly. Returning from a hunt, Jack sees Ralph and the others. He assumes his usual stature of bravura and mocks Ralph's attempts at regaining authority. Although Ralph accuses him of being a thief and their ensuing combat, Jack retains his position of power. He demonstrates this for all present by ordering that the twins be tied up. His hunters respond despite the twins' cries and Ralph's protests. Foolishly, Piggy insists on holding the conch while he criticizes their childlike behavior. This enrages Jack all the more. In the ensuing frenzy of screaming and yelling, no one notices Roger, who is levering a rock high above Piggy's head. The sound of it falling is heard before anyone sees it fall. Piggy's body, caught up in the force of the falling rock, falls silently to a flat red rock in the sea some forty feet below. Jack breaks the silence with another attack on Ralph. After being hit by Jack's spears, Ralph runs away to escape the inevitable onslaught.

In the **last chapter**, Ralph seeks refuge deep in the cover of the forest. He surveys his wounds and listens. He proceeds cautiously through the woods, stopping only to eat some fruit. As Ralph continues deeper into the forest, he comes across a pig's head stuck at the end of a spear. Fear and rage taking over, Ralph lashes out against the head, which falls to the ground in pieces. Ralph grabs the spear and runs off to seek shelter.

In the thickness of the foliage, Ralph rests briefly. He peers through the tangle of greenery and sees some hunters approaching. The movements of two in particular are familiar. He calls gently to the twins. Samneric approach him cautiously. They warn him of the upcoming hunt: he is to be the prey, the hunters will communicate with signals, and Roger has sharpened a stick at both ends to use in the attack. Samneric thrust some meat into Ralph's hand as they hurry to join the others. Ralph does not understand the meaning of Roger's foretold action and stops briefly to think, only to tense again when he hears others approaching. He creeps further into the thicket until he finds a spot that he considers safe. Sleep overtakes him quickly.

As the next morning begins, Ralph is awake to hear the approach of the tribe. From some farther distance he hears Roger's shouting and grunting as he levers rocks from the overhanging cliffs. A large one falls close to Ralph's hideaway. The next rock is so large that its fall lifts Ralph off the ground and bangs him down against the brambles. But the rock-tossing does not succeed in forcing the prey out into the open. Ralph hears vicious laughter and then the mention of smoke. He creeps again toward the thicker part of the forest. Thanks to the warnings of Samneric, he can follow the signals of the hunters. He can keep pace with them and outdistance them just enough. But then Ralph realizes that they have started a fire and that the fire will soon overrun the dense forest. He runs, hearing as he goes the voices of the hunters in frenzied pursuit. He stops and crouches to hide yet again, but this time the face of a hunter is there waiting. Ralph is speared. He leaps up and runs, through the opening, toward their shelters, running as much from the hunters as from the fire, which is about to consume the shelters. Ralph leaps and rolls to the sand, holding up a hand as if to fend off the next attack.

The change to the final scene is as extreme in its abruptness as the hunt is in its explicit terror. Ralph looks up expecting to see a spear, another hunter, or the approaching fire, only to see the figure of a white-clad naval officer, who greets Ralph kindly. After asking a few questions, the officer uncomfortably acknowledges Ralph's state of distress. The officer explains that his ship stopped to investigate after seeing the fire's smoke. Little by little, the other boys, still engaged in their brutal hunt, approach. Ralph slowly comprehends the reality of their rescue and the devastation caused by their savage new world. He breaks down into sobs of grief at the wreckage of their island and their innocence. ✤

—Elizabeth Beaudin
Yale University

List of Characters

Ralph is the first boy that the reader encounters. He becomes the leader of the group by a vote of the boys present. The token of his authority is a conch, found by Piggy along the beach. Ralph uses this to sound assembly. Although he considers himself ill-suited to speak in front of the group, with the aid of the conch and Piggy's steady encouragement, Ralph gradually gains the confidence needed for spontaneous speech. This same confidence is eventually undermined, however, by Jack and the formation of his splinter group.

Ralph loses the tenuous command he has over his own common sense and the group as the attraction of Jack's more primitive lifestyle catches on. With Piggy's reassurance, though, Ralph continues to appeal to the more rational side of the boys. As the events unfold, Ralph struggles helplessly first with the illogical, then tragic, direction that the events take. Finally, he finds himself completely ostracized and the target of Jack's terrorizing hunt.

Piggy, the marginalized boy of the group because he is fat and wears glasses, is like today's nerd in that he offers a rational explanation, usually unsolicited, for all he sees and hears. His intellectual perspective complements Ralph's leadership. By repeatedly reminding the group of the need to be found, Piggy represents the voice of reason so out of place in the boys' new space of tropical freedom. His insistence on logic and reason lead to tragic consequences.

Jack (Merridew), the leader of the choir, becomes the leader of the hunters and the instigator of the subsequent chaos. Of all the boys, Jack's position as head choirboy is the closest association in the group to recognized authority. Jack states this fact in so many words as he nominates himself for the position of leader, won instead by Ralph. A bright boy, Jack depends more on force, violence, and intimidation than on his own wits to usurp Ralph's position as leader. He is the revolutionary that establishes the new world order, so much a repetition of the unwanted order and discipline of the boys' former life at school.

Simon, a delicate child who is first noticed because he faints, possesses a sensitive, quiet perspective lacking in the others. With this, he sees and understands more, but also because of this he perishes violently. Simon appears content to explore the island on his own, contemplating the many new things the tropical environment has to offer. In doing so, he discovers a hiding place, and like the hideaway, Simon remains separated from the chaos but within dangerous reach of it. His second discovery provokes a tragic demise.

Sam 'n' Eric (a.k.a. Samneric; Sam, Eric) are twins who function as one, completing each other's half-sentences or speaking in unison. Their shift to Jack's group represents one last blow of betrayal for Ralph.

Roger, Maurice, et al. are the other older boys, from the choir and the general group, who eventually align themselves with Jack in lieu of Ralph. Roger distinguishes himself from the others as a sadist who reinforces Jack's regime by inflicting corporal punishment on any nonconformist.

The littluns are the smallest of boys and are usually not distinguished as individuals. As a group they are playful but subject to fearful fantasies. Percival, an exemplary littlun, recites his name and address whenever addressed by another.

The Beast (the snake-thing, the Beastie, the Lord of the Flies) takes on many imaginative forms, but has an explainable physical form.

The boy with the wine-colored scar is a littlun who reports the first sighting of the Beast and then is seen no more. His disappearance worries Ralph and Piggy but is ignored by Jack. ✤

Critical Views

Louis J. Halle on Tragedy and Heroism in *Lord of the Flies*

[Louis J. Halle (b. 1910), a scholar of American foreign policy and international relations, is professor emeritus at the Graduate Institute of International Studies in Geneva, Switzerland. His many publications include *Civilization and Foreign Policy: An Inquiry for Americans* (1955), *Men and Nations* (1962), and *The Ideological Imagination* (1972). In this review, Halle praises the tragedy and heroism of the scenario of *Lord of the Flies* but believes that the book has no overall point to make.]

The oldest of the English schoolboys was twelve and the youngest six. Finding themselves plane-wrecked on an uninhabited tropical island, without grownups, they had to manage for themselves. English political experience since Runnymede, however, made its contribution. An assembly was called, a leader elected, rules established, assignments distributed. Civilization had come down out of the sky with the children.

But so had savagery, and fear of the unknown brought it out. Parliamentary procedure, after all, cannot propitiate the beast in the dark. For that you have to paint your face with colored clays, chant incantations, dance ritualistically, and offer blood sacrifices. So the struggle between civilization and barbarism began.

William Golding tells all this in his first novel, *Lord of the Flies.* One is impressed by the possibilities of his theme for an expression of the irony and tragedy of man's fate. Against his majority of little savages he places a remnant that convincingly represents the saving element of human heroism, thereby posing the eternal moral conflict. But he cannot quite find his meaning in this material. The heroes come to a bad end, having contributed nothing to such salvation as the society achieves. There is a great deal of commotion, and the last page is nothing more than a playwright's contrivance for bringing down the curtain. One is left asking: What was the point?

—Louis J. Halle, "Small Savages," *Saturday Review,* 15 October 1955, p. 16

✤

THE *TIMES LITERARY SUPPLEMENT* ON REALISM AND HORROR IN *LORD OF THE FLIES*

[In this anonymous review of *Lord of the Flies* in Britain's leading review journal, the *Times Literary Supplement,* the reviewer finds that the horror of the situation in the novel resides precisely in its realism—in the possibility that such a situation could actually occur.]

The story is fantastic in conception and setting: but with so much of strangeness granted, *Lord of the Flies,* like all successful fantasies, enlightens and horrifies by its nearness to, rather than its distance from, reality. Accept the idea of children being set down on an island in conditions that preclude the possibility of starvation, and this is really how they might behave. A leader is elected, Ralph; a boy honest, tenacious, not highly intelligent but aware that the first requirements are to build shelters and to keep a fire burning day and night. A routine of duties is arranged; there will be fire stokers, shelter builders, hunting parties to catch pigs. But the routine becomes tiresome and is not maintained; the smaller children believe that there is a beast in the forest, and it is only one step from belief in the beast to worship of it, one step more to the idea that the beast must be propitiated by a human sacrifice. A new chief is chosen who fulfils the children's desire for a reversion to primitivism, and the old chief becomes in the natural course of things a scapegoat.

Perhaps this makes *Lord of the Flies* sound too much like a variation on a Frazerian theme. It is that, incidentally; but taken purely as a story it is beautifully constructed and worked out, with the various children just sufficiently individuated and with tension built up steadily to the climax in which the scapegoat is hunted over the island.

—Unsigned, "Tales of Imagination," *Times Literary Supplement*, 22 October 1955, p. 669

FRANK KERMODE ON UNINTENDED MEANINGS IN *LORD OF THE FLIES*

[Frank Kermode (b. 1919), one of the leading British critics of the century, is King Edward VII Professor of English at King's College, Cambridge. His many publications include *The Sense of an Ending* (1967), *Poetry, Narrative, History* (1990), and *The Uses of Error* (1991). In this extract, Kermode believes that some elements of *Lord of the Flies* have broader meanings not encompassed by Golding's conscious designs for the book.]

Lord of the Flies was 'worked out carefully in every possible way', and its author holds that the 'programme' of the book *is* its meaning. He rejects ⟨D. H.⟩ Lawrence's doctrine, 'Never trust the artist, trust the tale' and its consequence, 'the proper function of the critic is to save the tale from the artist'. He is wrong, I think; in so far as the book differs from its programme there is, as a matter of common sense, material over which the writer has no absolute authority. This means not only that there are possible readings which he cannot veto, but even that some of his own views on the book may be in a sense wrong. The interpretation of the dead parachutist is an example. This began in the 'programme' as straight allegory; Golding says that this dead man 'is' History. 'All that we can give our children' in their trouble is this monstrous dead adult, who's 'dead, but won't lie down'; an ugly emblem of war and decay that broods over the paradise and provides the only objective equivalent for the beast the boys imagine. Now this limited allegory (I may even have expanded it in the telling) seems to me not to have got out of the 'programme' into the book; what does get in is more valuable because more like myth—capable, that is, of more various interpretation than the rigidity of Golding's scheme allows. And in writing of this kind all depends upon the author's mythopoeic power to transcend the 'programme'.

—Frank Kermode, "William Golding" (1958–60), *Puzzles and Epiphanies: Essays and Reviews 1958–1961* (New York: Chilmark, 1962), pp. 204–5

✣

PETER GREEN ON GOLDING'S SYMBOLISM

[Peter Green (b. 1924) is a prolific British critic and classical scholar. Among his many books are *Kenneth Grahame: A Biography* (1959), *Alexander the Great* (1970), and *The Shadow of the Parthenon* (1972). He is currently a professor of classics at the University of Texas. In this extract, Green traces the symbolism in *The Lord of the Flies,* which gives the novel a more universal significance beyond its political message.]

At one level *Lord of the Flies* portrays a gradual reversion to the most primitive and bloodthirsty savagery. To begin with, the children impose 'civilised' standards of conduct on their small community. They elect a leader, Ralph. They have a meeting-place for discussions, and a conch-shell to summon them. This conch also becomes a symbol of rational behaviour: no one may speak unless he is holding it. And here, already, the percipient reader gets his first twinge of uneasiness, remembering that a similar habit prevailed among Homer's heroes: these young boys are slipping back on the path that leads to primitivism.

Gradually the shibboleths of twentieth-century civilisation are erased from these middle-class boys' minds. First come irrational fears: of imaginary monsters and the numinous unknown. Then the boys split into two groups: the hunters, and those struggling to retain their civilised standards. The hunters, their initial squeamishness lost, revel in the blood-lust induced by pig-sticking. It is characteristic of the hunters that they loathe and despise those who will not join them. Two of these, Piggy and Simon, are murdered; the third, Ralph himself, is hunted across the island, and only saved by the opportune arrival of a Royal Navy landing-party.

Behind this main narrative structure, as always in Golding's work, we find more universal moral implications. What Ralph weeps for, on the last page, is 'the end of innocence, the darkness of man's heart'. Piggy will have no truck with the group-consciousness, and because of this he is killed. Here the book reveals a terrifying microcosm of political totalitarianism. With Simon we are at a deeper level still. Simon is a saint, mystic and clairvoyant. It is Simon, and Simon alone, who sees the others' fear and superstition for what they are. This point is made by the use of two very explicit symbols: the Beast, and the Lord of the Flies himself.

The Beast, to begin with, is nothing more than a focal point for the boys' vague, archaic fears. Later the Beast is given a spurious reality: the corpse of an airman, still harnessed to its parachute, drifts down from some aerial battle on to the beacon hill at the top of the island. Two children see it in the dark, and instantly the myth of terror is established. But Simon is incredulous: 'however Simon thought of the Beast, there rose before his inward sight the picture of a human at once heroic and sick.'

Meanwhile Jack, whose instinct tells him the Beast must be placated, erects a pole in the forest with a pig's head stuck on top of it as an offering. Simon, walking alone, stumbles on this totemic emblem, buzzing with flies, and instantly, instinctively, knows it for what it is. The more sophisticated reader quickly works out the equation. Baalzebub was the Philistine Lord of Flies; the Jews transmuted his name to mean Lord of Dung or Filth; by the time of the New Testament he was Lord of the Devils, a generalised Satan. It is this potent deity with whom Simon has his strange conversation in the jungle:

> Simon's head was tilted slightly up. His eyes could not break away and the Lord of the Flies hung in space before him.
>
> 'What are you doing out here all alone? Aren't you afraid of me?'

> Simon shook.
>
> 'There isn't anyone to help you. Only me. And I'm the Beast.'
>
> Simon's mouth laboured, brought forth audible words.
>
> 'Pig's head on a stick.'
>
> 'Fancy thinking the Beast was something you could hunt and kill!' said the head. For a moment or two the forest and all the other dimly appreciated places echoed with the parody of laughter. 'You knew, didn't you? I'm part of you.'

In other words, it is man who creates his own hell, his own devils; the evil is in him.

—Peter Green, "The World of William Golding," *Review of English Literature* 1, No. 2 (April 1960): 65–66

James Gindin on the Ending of *Lord of the Flies* as a Gimmick

[James Gindin (b. 1926), a professor of English at the University of Michigan, is the author of *Post-War British Fiction* (1962), *William Golding* (1988), and *British Fiction in the 1930s: The Dispiriting Decade* (1992). In this extract, Gindin criticizes the ending of *Lord of the Flies* as a gimmick or trick that undermines the power of the moral parable.]

Golding's first novel, *Lord of the Flies,* tells the story of a group of English schoolboys, between the ages of six and twelve, who survive a plane crash on a tropical island. The boys were apparently evacuated during a destructive atomic war and are left with no adult control anywhere about, to build their own society on the island. The chance to create a new Paradise is clear enough, but Golding quickly indicates that the boys are products of and intrinsically parts of current human society. Even on the very first page: "The fair boy stopped and jerked his stockings with an automatic gesture that made the jungle seem for a moment like the Home Counties." The island provides food, plenty of opportunity for swimming, and "fun." But a conflict quickly develops between the boys, led by Ralph, who would keep a fire going (they cherish some hope of rescue) and build adequate shelters and those, led by Jack, originally members of a choir, who would hunt wild pigs and give full reign to their predatory and savage instincts. In the first, democratic, meeting, Ralph wins most of the boys' votes, is elected the leader of the island. But the rational democracy is not able to cope very well with the fears of the younger boys, the occasional tendency to rash mob action, the terror of the unexplained "beast" that fills the night. Gradually, Jack gains more followers. He paints himself in savage colors, neglects to tend the fire because he is mercilessly tracking down a wild pig, establishes a wild and ritualistic dance that fascinates the boys. When one of the boys, having discovered the rational truth of the "beast" at the top of the mountain (the "beast" is a dead man in his parachute; dropped from a battle ten miles above the island), stumbles into the ritualistic dance, he is forced by Jack to enact the role of the pig. The boy is never given the time or the opportunity to make the rational truth clear, for the dancers, cloaked in frenzy and darkness, kill him. Ralph is unable to stop the others, even, to his shame, recognizes some of the same dark frenzy at the center of his own being. And Piggy, Ralph's "brain trust" though always unattractive and unpopular, the boy whose glasses got the fire going in the first place, is killed by Jack's principal lieutenant. Jack is victorious. His dogmatic authority, his cruelty, and his barbaric frenzy have a deeper hold on the nature of man than do Ralph's sensible regulations. The forces of light and reason fail to alleviate the predatory brutality and the dark, primeval fear at the center of man.

But the metaphor of the society the boys construct is not left to do its work alone. Just when the savage forces led by Jack are tracking down Ralph and burning the whole island to find him, a British naval officer arrives to rescue the boys. Ironically, the smoke of barbaric fury, not the smoke of conscious effort, has led to rescue. Throughout the novel, frequent references to possible rescue and to the sanity of the adult world seemed the delusions of the rational innocent. Ralph and Piggy often appealed to adult sanity in their futile attempt to control their world, but, suddenly and inconsistently at the end of the novel, adult sanity really exists. The horror of the boys' experience on the island was really a childish game, though a particularly vicious one, after all. The British officer turns into a public school master: "I should have thought that a pack of British boys—you're all British aren't you?—would have been able to put up a better show than that." The officer's density is apparent, but the range of the whole metaphor has been severely limited. Certainly, the whole issue, the whole statement about man is not contradicted by the ending, for, as Golding directly points out, Ralph has learned from the experience: "And in the middle of them, with filthy body, matted hair, and unwiped nose, Ralph wept for the end of innocence, the darkness of man's heart, and the fall through the air of the true, wise friend called Piggy." But the rescue is ultimately a "gimmick," a trick, a means of cutting down or softening the implications built up within the structure of the boys' society on the island.

—James Gindin, "'Gimmick' and Metaphor in the Novels of William Golding," *Modern Fiction Studies* 6, No. 2 (Summer 1960): 145–47

CARL NIEMEYER ON *LORD OF THE FLIES* CONTRASTED WITH *CORAL ISLAND*

[Carl Niemeyer, an author and translator, is a former professor of English and chairman of the Division of the Humanities at Union College. In this extract, Niemeyer compares *Lord of the Flies* with R. M. Ballantyne's *The Coral Island,* finding Golding's novel far more realistic than Ballantyne's, even though the message behind it is dispiriting.]

The distance we have travelled from Ballantyne's cheerful unrealities is both artistic and moral. Golding is admittedly symbolic; Ballantyne professed to be telling a true story. Yet it is the symbolic tale that, at least for our times, carries conviction. Golding's boys, who choose to remember nothing of their past before the plane accident; who, as soon as Jack commands the choir to take off the robes marked with the cross of Christianity, have no trace of religion; who demand to be ruled and are incapable of being ruled properly; who though many of them were once choir boys (Jack could sing C sharp) never sing a note on the island; in whose minds the great tradition of Western culture has left the titles of a few books for children, a knowledge of the use of matches (but no matches), and hazy memories of planes and TV sets—these boys are more plausible than Ballantyne's. His was a world of blacks and whites: bad hurricanes, good islands; good pigs obligingly allowing themselves to be taken for human food, bad sharks disobligingly taking human beings for shark food; good Christians, bad natives; bad pirates, good boys. Of the beast within, which demands blood sacrifice, first a sow's head, then a boy's, Ballantyne has some vague notion, but he cannot take it seriously. Not only does Golding see the beast; he sees that to keep it at bay we have civilization; but when by some magic or accident civilization is abolished and the human animal is left on his own, dependent upon his mere humanity, then being human is not enough. The beast appears, though not necessarily spontaneously or inevitably, for it never rages in Ralph or Piggy or Simon as it does in Roger or Jack; but it is latent in all of them, in the significantly named Piggy, in Ralph, who sometimes envies the abandon of the hunters and who shares the desire to "get a handful" of Robert's "brown, vulnerable flesh," and even in Simon burrowing into his private hiding place. After Simon's death Jack attracts all the boys but Ralph and the loyal Piggy into his army. Then when Piggy is killed and Ralph is alone, only civilization can save him. The timely arrival of the British Navy is less theatrical than logically necessary to make Golding's point. For civilization defeats the beast. It slinks back into the jungle as the boys creep out to be rescued; but the beast is real. It is there, and it may return.

—Carl Niemeyer, "The Coral Island Revisited," *College English* 22, No. 4 (January 1961): 244–45

E. M. Forster on Golding's Partial Christianity

[E. M. Forster (1879–1970), one of the most important British novelists of the twentieth century, was also a leading critic and reviewer. Among his critical works are *Abinger Harvest* (1924) and *Aspects of the Novel* (1927). In this extract, Forster detects that Golding in *Lord of the Flies* is a Christian in his acknowledgment of at least the possibility of original sin, but he has not included the notion of a Redeemer.]

The hideous accidents that promote the reversion to savagery fill most of the book, and the reader must be left to endure them—and also to embrace them, for somehow or other they are entangled with beauty. The greatness of the vision transcends what is visible. At the close, when the boys are duly rescued by the trim British cruiser, we find ourselves on their side. We have shared their experience and resent the smug cheeriness of their rescuers. The naval officer is a bit disappointed with what he finds—everyone filthy dirty, swollen bellies, faces daubed with clay, two missing at least and the island afire. It ought to have been more like Coral Island, he suggests.

> Ralph looked at him dumbly. For a moment he had a fleeting picture of the strange glamour that had once invested the beaches. But the island was scorched up like dead wood—Simon was dead—and Jack had . . . The tears began to flow and sobs shook him. He gave himself up to them now for the first time on the island; great, shuddering spasms of grief that seemed to wrench his whole body. His voice rose under the black smoke before the burning wreckage of the island; and infected by that emotion, the other little boys began to shake and sob too. And in the middle of them, with filthy body, matted hair, and unwiped nose, Ralph wept for the end of innocence, the darkness of man's heart, and the fall through the air of the true, wise friend called Piggy.

This passage—so pathetic—is also revealing. Phrases like "the end of innocence" and "the darkness of man's heart" show us the author's attitude more clearly than has appeared hitherto. He believes in the Fall of Man and perhaps in Original Sin. Or if he does not exactly believe, he fears; the same fear infects his second novel, a difficult and profound work called *The*

Inheritors. Here the innocent (the boys as it were) are Neanderthal Man, and the corrupters are Homo Sapiens, our own ancestors, who eat other animals, discover intoxicants, and destroy. Similar notions occur in his other novels.

Thus his attitude approaches the Christian: we are all born in sin, or will all lapse into it. But he does not complete the Christian attitude, for the reason that he never introduces the idea of a Redeemer. When a deity does appear, he is the Lord of the Flies, Beelzebub, and he sends a messenger to prepare his way before him.

—E. M. Forster, "Introduction," *Lord of the Flies* by William Golding (New York: Coward-McCann, 1962), pp. xi–xii

✤

WILLIAM GOLDING ON THE PURPOSE OF *LORD OF THE FLIES*

[William Golding's most detailed statement of the purpose behind his writing of *Lord of the Flies* occurs in a lecture entitled "Fable." Here, Golding declares that the fundamental message in the novel is a philosophical exposition of the notion that "man is a fallen being." He goes on to describe two of the central characters of the book, Ralph and Simon.]

Man is a fallen being. He is gripped by original sin. His nature is sinful and his state perilous. I accept the theology and admit the triteness; but what is trite is true; and a truism can become more than a truism when it is a belief passionately held. I looked round me for some convenient form in which this thesis might be worked out, and found it in the play of children. I was well situated for this, since at this time I was teaching them. Moreover, I am a son, brother, and father. I have lived for many years with small boys, and understand and know them with awful precision. I decided to take the literary convention of boys on an island, only make them real boys instead of paper cutouts with no life in them; and try to show how the shape of the society they evolved would be conditioned by their diseased, their fallen nature. ⟨. . .⟩

The protagonist was Ralph, the average, rather more than average, man of goodwill and commonsense; the man who makes mistakes because he simply does not understand at first the nature of the disease from which they all suffer. The boys find an earthly paradise, a world, in fact like our world, of boundless wealth, beauty and resource. The boys were below the age of overt sex, for I did not want to complicate the issue with that relative triviality. They did not have to fight for survival, for I did not want a Marxist exegesis. If disaster came, it was not to come through the exploitation of one class by another. It was to rise, simply and solely out of the nature of the brute. The overall picture was to be the tragic lesson that the English have had to learn over a period of one hundred years; that one lot of people is inherently like any other lot of people; and that the only enemy of man is inside him.

⟨. . .⟩ For reasons it is not necessary to specify, I included a Christ-figure in my fable. This is the little boy Simon, solitary, stammering, a lover of mankind, a visionary, who reaches commonsense attitudes not by reason but by intuition. Of all the boys, he is the only one who feels the need to be alone and goes every now and then into the bushes. Since this book is one that is highly and diversely explicable, you would not believe the various interpretations that have been given of Simon's going into the bushes. But go he does, and prays, as the child Jean Vianney would go, and some other saints—though not many. He is really turning a part of the jungle into a church, not a physical one, perhaps, but a spiritual one. Here there is a scene, when civilization has already begun to break down under the combined pressures of boy-nature and the thing still ducking and bowing on the mountaintop, when the hunters bring before him, without knowing he is there, their false god, the pig's head on a stick. It was at this point of imaginative concentration that I found that the pig's head knew Simon was there. In fact the Pig's head delivered something very like a sermon to the boy; the pig's head spoke. I know because I heard it.

—William Golding, "Fable," *The Hot Gates and Other Occasional Pieces* (New York: Harcourt, Brace & World, 1965), pp. 88–89, 97–98

✤

Bernard S. Oldsey and Stanley Weintraub on the Overlap Between Fiction and Allegory

[Bernard S. Oldsey (b. 1923), a professor of English at West Chester State College, is the author of *British Novelists 1930–1959* (1983) and editor of *Critical Essays on George Orwell* (1986). Stanley Weintraub (b. 1929), a leading scholar on George Bernard Shaw, is a professor of English at Pennsylvania State University and the author of *Lawrence of Arabia: The Literary Impulse* (1975) and *Beardsley: A Biography* (1975). In this extract from their book on Golding, Oldsey and Weintraub find the chief merit of *Lord of the Flies* in its treading the boundary between allegory and fiction: the incidents have the feel of realism, but are placed in a vague and unspecified time and place.]

The scenic qualities of *Lord of the Flies* help make it an imaginative work for the reader as well as the author. Although Golding occasionally provides consolidating detail, he more commonly requires the reader to pull narrative and descriptive elements into focus. For example, he provides no end-paper map or block description of his fictional island. The reader must explore it along with the participants in the story and piece together a usable concept of time and place. What we learn in this way is just enough to keep the work within the realm of fiction, but not enough to remove it from the realm of allegory. *And the essence of Golding's art resides exactly within the area of overlap.*

Fable-like, time and place are vague. The Queen (Elizabeth?) still reigns, and "Reds" are apparently the vague enemy. It is the postcatastrophic near-future, in which nuclear war has laid waste much of the West. ("They're all dead," Piggy thinks. And "civilization," corroborates Golding, is "in ruins.") The fiery crash of the boys' plane upon a tropical island has been the final stage of their evacuation from England. The island seems to lie somewhere in the Indian or Pacific Ocean, probably on a line extending from England to Australia, which could well have been the planned terminus of their evacuation. Jack provides the clue for such geographical extrapolation when he speaks of Simon's seizures at "Gib." (Gibraltar) and "Addis" (Addis Ababa), as well as "at matins over the precentor." ⟨. . .⟩

When the details are extracted and given order under an analytical light, Golding's island looks naturalistic in specification. But matters are not at all that clear in the book. The location of the island, for example, is kept deliberately vague: it is sufficiently remote to draw only two ships in a month or so, yet close enough to "civilization" to be the floor above which deadly, and old-fashioned, air battles are fought miles high (the boys' plane itself has been shot down). The nearby air and naval war in progress, with conventional weapons, is somewhat out of keeping with earlier reports of utter catastrophe. Equally incongruous is the smartly attired naval officer and savior of the closing pages, whose jaunty mien is incompatible with catastrophe. Yet he is as important to the machinery of the allegory as the earlier crash, which is equally difficult to explain on rational grounds. During the crash the fuselage of the evacuation plane has apparently broken in two: the forward half (holding pilot and others, including more boys) has been cleanly washed out to sea by a conveniently concomitant storm; and the after-section (which makes a long fiery scar as it cuts through the jungle) tumbles unscathed children onto the island. As incompatible, obscure, askew, and unrealistic as these elements may be, they are no more so than Gulliver's adventures. And Golding's graphically novelistic character and topographic details, both poetic and naturalistic, tend to blur the fabulous qualities of the narrative's use of time and setting in its opening and close. Although it is enough to say that the fabulist must be permitted pegs upon which to hang his fable, it is Golding's richly novelistic elements of the telling that call attention to the subtle dissonance. Paradoxically—yet artistically—this very tension between realistic novel and allegorical fable imparts to *Lord of the Flies* some of its unique power.

—Bernard S. Oldsey and Stanley Weintraub, *The Art of William Golding* (New York: Harcourt, Brace & World, 1965), pp. 17–20

✤

BERNARD F. DICK ON GOLDING'S USE OF BEELZEBUB

[Bernard F. Dick (b. 1935), a professor at Fairleigh Dickinson University, is the author of *Anatomy of Film* (1978), *Billy Wilder* (1980), and *Hellman in Hollywood* (1982). In this extract from his book on Golding, Dick studies the figure of Beelzebub in *Lord of the Flies,* tracing the symbolism of the "lord of the flies" throughout the work.]

Sooner or later, the reader must confront the meaning of the title which, like all of Golding's symbolism, is linked with the events of the novel. Thus, even for purposes of discussion, it cannot be isolated from the action. "Lord of the flies" is a translation of *Beelzebub,* the Greek transliteration of the Hebrew *Ba'alzevuv,* and in Judaism and Christianity denotes the principle of evil personified—the Devil, Satan, Mephistopheles. Golding equates the "Lord of the Flies" with the demonic force latent in man; it is generally kept in check by the rational part of human nature, but in the absence of reason or social pressure, breaks out in an act of barbaric bloodletting. This force has been called by a variety of names, depending upon whether one is a theologian, a poet, or a humanist: original sin, "Adam's Curse," "the darkness of man's heart," "The Banality of Evil." To the realist the demonic is merely a corollary of the theorem of existence; as a concomitant of human nature, it cannot be ignored, and only the saint can surmount it by asceticism.

Golding does not immediately symbolize his philosophy of evil, but in his usual way allows it to flow from a series of events. First, the "littluns" complain of seeing an imaginary beast; the fear that has grown out of their fitful imaginations, which must attach itself to an object, finds an outlet in the dead paratrooper. The hunters, who revert to the most primitive form of expiation, transfix the head of a slain pig on a pole as a blood offering to the "beast." Simon comes upon the impaled head, and his confrontation with it is dramatically heralded by the disappearance of the butterflies.

The insect-covered head introduces itself as the "Lord of the Flies," an expression which, like so much in Golding, is ironically accurate. The "adult cynicism" which it imparts to Simon is significant, for the young seer has directly confronted evil without the assuring barricade of butterflies: " 'Fancy thinking the Beast was something you could hunt and kill!' said the head. For a moment or two the forest and all the other dimly appreciated places echoed with the parody of laughter. 'You knew, didn't you? I'm part of you? Close, close, close! I'm the reason why it's no go? Why things are what they are?' "

Simon has communed with evil concretely embodied in a pig's head buzzing with flies, and the proximity causes him to faint. He had fainted once before when the black-robed choristers entered and cast a dark shadow on the coral island. He faints now because he has received knowledge too overwhelming to endure.

Golding's Lord of the Flies is not the biblical Satan who tempts Christ, nor the Miltonic counterpart who speaks in glorious rhetoric. Rather it is a pig's head—evil reduced to one of its vilest incarnations. Golding will have nothing to do with a suave Mephistopheles or a honey-tongued Lucifer; his Devil is more in keeping with Dorian Gray's decaying portrait because it abandons rhetorical finery for the stark reality of spiritual corruption. The Lord of the Flies was correct: the beast is in man; and, when it expresses itself, it is in the form of a rotting self-portrait.

—Bernard F. Dick, *William Golding* (New York: Twayne, 1967), pp. 27–28

Mark Kinkead-Weekes and Ian Gregor on the Saintliness of Simon

[Mark Kinkead-Weekes (b. 1931), a professor of English at the University of Kent in Canterbury, England, is the editor of *Twentieth-Century Interpretations of* The Rainbow (1971). Ian Gregor is the editor of *The Brontës: A Collection of Critical Essays* (1970) and

Reading the Victorian Novel (1980). In this extract from their book on Golding, Kinkead-Weekes and Gregor examine the prophetic nature of Simon and his sensitivity to the beauty and terror of the island.]

There is something saintly in Simon; but such labelling accomplishes far less than one might imagine. What brings Simon alive is not good works, or prayer, or faith, or a personal relationship with his creator, and a ten or eleven year old is a slender reed to bear the symbolic weight of saint, let alone of Saviour. This kind of reading will not stand up to examination. What does, demonstrably, bring Simon alive and make the passages where he is by himself among the finest things in the book, is the quality of the imagination that goes into creating his particular sensibility. He is not so much a character, in the sense that the other boys are, as the most inclusive sensibility among the children at this stage.

The presentation of Simon in this chapter is not as symbolic as we think when it starts, and not symbolic at all as it goes on. Those littluns, if we look at them, are 'unintelligible' and 'inscrutable', not paradisal. The flowers and fruit raise the question of Eden, certainly, but they also come direct from *Coral Island,* and represent simple physical fact in the South Seas where many fruit trees bear all the year round. Moreover the enormous fecundity, 'the scent of ripeness and the booming of a million bees at pasture', will strike most readers as excessive for Eden.

This assertive fecundity sets the tone of the scene as it develops. What strikes us with considerable force, as Simon moves through the jungle, is that it is alien to man, and the way that its fecundity is rooted in dissolution. The pale flowers parasitic on the tall trunks are 'unexpected' by the civilized eye; the birds not only 'bright' but 'fantastic'. In the treetops life goes on 'clamorously'; the clearing below is an 'aromatic . . . bowl of heat and light'; the 'rapid' climber 'flaunted' red and yellow blossoms; the butterflies are 'gaudy', the colours 'riotous'. Underfoot the soil is markedly soft, and 'the creepers shivered throughout their lengths when he bumped them'. They are dropped 'like the rigging of foundered ships', and the climber is parasitic on a great tree that has fallen and died. This, clearly enough if we look, is no Eden and never was; there was no death in Eden, no riot or urgency, no creepiness.

Simon is the first child to know, to register fully, what the island and its jungle are like in themselves. The qualities that were present in Ralph's daydreaming at the finding of the conch, but have subsequently been overlaid by his need to think and lead, are fully realized in Simon. On the other hand, in solitary communion with nature, he taps Jack's sensitivity to the creepy as well as the beautiful. But he is outside the hunter mentality, the leader mentality, outside even himself. He exists in terms of his sensitivity to what is outside him. This allows him to know comprehensively. He not only registers the heat, the urgency, the riot, the dampness and decay; he also registers the cool and mysterious submergence of the forest in darkness, the pure beauty and fragrance of starlight and nightflower, the peace. Finally he not only registers both, but accepts them equally, as two parts of the same reality. It is these qualities of acceptance and inclusion that give us the 'Simon-ness' of Simon.

—Mark Kinkead-Weekes and Ian Gregor, *William Golding: A Critical Study* (London: Faber & Faber, 1967), pp. 29–31

✤

HOWARD S. BABB ON THE DETERIORATION OF SOCIETY IN *LORD OF THE FLIES*

[Howard S. Babb (1924–1978) was a professor of English at the University of California at Irvine. He wrote *Jane Austen's Novels: The Fabric of Dialogue* (1962) and edited *Essays in Stylistic Analysis* (1972). In this extract from his book on Golding, Babb studies the society that the castaway boys form around the two leaders, Jack and Ralph, and its rapid deterioration into lawlessness.]

As our cue to reviewing *Lord of the Flies* in its main outline, we may take Golding's statement that the book deals in part with "the defects of society." For the group of boys who find themselves on an uninhabited island—as the result of a plane crash during their evacuation from England in an atomic war—try to create a society for themselves, but experience its disintegration. The society begins to come into being when Ralph blows the conch he has discovered, the children collecting on the beach. But already there is a hint of irresponsibility in the pleasure the young ones feel at the notion of "something purposeful being done"—by others (Ralph is sounding the conch, and Piggy gathering names)—a pleasure underscored by the action of one who starts sucking his thumb. At the first assembly, the group exercises what Golding terms the "toy of voting" to elect Ralph chief, attracted to him not by any "good reason" but by his possession of the conch. When, after the island has been explored, Ralph guides the second assembly toward determining to light a signal fire for facilitating rescue, the group bolts off after Jack—Ralph's defeated rival for the position of chief, the leader of the choirboys designated by Jack himself as this society's "hunters"—and kindles a blaze that burns up part of the island, moves the children to delight and "awe at the power" they have "set free," and causes the first death on the island.

Society's attempt to build shelters proves as ineffective as its effort to keep a signal fire going. Only Ralph and Simon are still on the job when Golding first shows us this world at work, the other children having drifted off to doing whatever they enjoy, with Jack devoting himself to mastering a technique for hunting pigs. The split between Jack and Ralph, discernible when they met initially, starts to emerge as a split between different organizing principles of society (among other things) when Ralph complains that Jack hunts because he likes to, "You want to hunt," while implying that he himself builds from a sense of duty. If the pleasures of some older children reveal their irresponsibility and latent cruelty—in one scene, Roger and Maurice kick over the sandcastles of the "littluns," Roger then throwing stones to frighten a child on the shore—Golding insists that the same qualities inhere in the "littluns" themselves, one of whom keeps throwing sand at his crying playmate, while another basks in the joy of "exercising control over [the] living things" at the waterline and "ordering them."

Appropriately enough, the first killing of a pig, which both gratifies Jack's dark pleasure in hunting and marks the initial success of the children in having "imposed their will" on "a living thing," costs society a chance to be rescued, for the hunters have abandoned the signal fire as a ship passes the island—and Jack smashes one lens of Piggy's glasses, the instrument of the society for lighting its signal fire, when he is rebuked for the hunters' irresponsibility.

The assembly that ensues, called by Ralph in part for the purpose of "deciding on the fear" which afflicts the children, dissolves into a confused dance when the children testify that they are indeed haunted. And soon their fear is embodied in the dead airman—civilization's ironic response to Ralph's wish for some stabilizing "sign" from the world of grownups—who parachutes to the island to become "the beast" in the eyes of this society. The expedition that Ralph organizes in the service of the group to discover whether the reported beast really exists, an expedition led at many moments by Jack, is itself sidetracked for a time into a hunt and dance, Ralph participating in both. Once the presence of the beast is validated—once society has thus enthroned its evil—Jack openly challenges Ralph for the position of chief in an assembly which Jack himself has called, departing to found a society of hunters himself when the group fails to support him formally.

—Howard S. Babb, *The Novels of William Golding* (Columbus: Ohio State University Press, 1970), pp. 8–10

DAVID H. RICHTER ON THE ENDING OF *LORD OF THE FLIES*

[David H. Richter (b. 1945) is a professor of English at Queen's College and author of *Ten Short Novels* (1980) and *Fable's End* (1974), from which the following extract is taken. Here, Richter challenges the view of James Gindin that the ending of *Lord of the Flies* is a "gimmick," believing that it is meant to be interpreted symbolically.]

The question of the inconsistency of the ending has in one sense already been answered by Golding himself: "The officer having interrupted a manhunt, prepares to take the children off the island in a cruiser which will presently be hunting its enemy in the same implacable way. And who will rescue the adult and his cruiser?" We shall go into this statement in greater detail shortly. But if what Gindin means to say is that the ending brings about an abrupt shift from the "symbolic" to the "naturalistic" mode of narration, Golding's commentaries seem to lend him support, especially where he says that "the whole book is symbolic in nature except the rescue in the end." I can see an abrupt shift in point of view, even in frame of reference, but I am afraid I cannot take the rescuing officer and his gunboat as any more or less symbolic in nature than the boys themselves and their society. In fact, I find rather confusing the notion that "naturalistic" sailors could rescue "symbolic" children: by the last pages of the novel, it would be difficult for the reader to take any newly introduced character or event as simply self-referential.

And Golding's detail helps us work out the significance of the rescue. The officer, with "white-topped cap. . . . white drill, epaulettes, a revolver, a row of gilt buttons," is a kindly fellow—so it seems from his conversation—but he does not take "his hand away from the butt of his revolver" until he sees that the little boys pose no threat to him; but the sailors had come expecting trouble—witness the petty officer in the stern of the cutter holding a submachine gun ready for action. The rescuers who stop the island war are themselves men of war, as Golding says, "dignified and capable, but in reality enmeshed in the same evil" we have seen in all the children: the viciousness and savagery of human nature. War is one manifestation of this "evil," and crime, of course, would be another; all the sad variety of human life in which man's inhumanity to man, the "darkness of man's heart," is revealed bears witness to the truth about the adult world for which the "friendly" sailors stand as symbols. There is no shift to the naturalistic mode, although, as Drew put it, "the eye is . . . taken away from the microscope." By the introduction of actual adults, Golding's symbolic narrative is broadened to include the grownup world about which the children had metaphorically been speaking all along. The mode of their introduction underlines the truth of Golding's thesis respecting them. The "microscope" becomes a wide-angle lens. This is the answer, then, to our second question: far from tending "to simplify and palliate" the experience, the denouement broadens and extends beyond its own immediate significance the morality play which has been enacted on the island. "The darkness of man's heart" is not evinced merely by the slackening of the bonds of civilization; it is not to be found only on coral islands: it is, in fact, always with us, the ultimate source of all human pain and misery.

—David H. Richter, "Allegory versus Fable: Golding's *Lord of the Flies,*" *Fable's End: Completeness and Closure in Rhetorical Fiction* (Chicago: University of Chicago Press, 1974), pp. 75–76

ANDREW SINCLAIR ON SEA SYMBOLISM IN *LORD OF THE FLIES*

[Andrew Sinclair (b. 1935) is a prolific British novelist, biographer, and historian. Among his works are *The Savage: A History of Misunderstanding* (1977) and biographies of Dylan Thomas (1975), Jack London (1977), and Edgar Allan Poe (1979). In this extract, Sinclair traces the symbolism of the sea throughout Golding's work and especially in *Lord of the Flies,* where it represents both positive and negative qualities.]

Often seen as a paradigm of the breakdown of society, a myth of the fall from innocence and of the exposure of savagery under the civilized skin, the novel is also a profound examination of the relationship between the sea and human beings. The situation is, of course, taken from *Coral Island,* and the boys are wrecked on an isolated tropical place, bordered on its four corners by the ocean. At first, the sea represents pleasure, holiday, relief and reassurance. The deep bathing pool with its ledge of pink granite is warmer than blood, a huge bath, and it comforts

Ralph and Piggy. They are persuaded that a ship will soon come to rescue them, possibly captained by Ralph's father, a commander in the Navy. Familiar authority governs the seas; for English boys, Britannia rules the waves. No island is unknown. The Queen is believed to have a room full of maps, on which every island is drawn. Sooner or later, paternity and adult security will appear to rescue the castaway boys.

This is, indeed, what happens in the end. The beginning of Ralph's confrontation with Jack and his hunters is when the fire is left to go out, a ship passes by, and a slaughtered wild pig is the antithesis of orderly rescue. Finally, when savagery has taken over and Ralph himself has become the quarry and victim, he is saved by the sudden appearance of a naval officer, *deus ex nave,* landing in his cutter from a trim cruiser in the distance. Ralph weeps for the end of innocence and the darkness of man's heart and the death of Piggy, but he survives because of the necessary authority of those who must navigate on the oceans.

The reef is also the second barrier to the sea that creates a preliminary Eden for the wrecked boys. Inside the coral limits, the water is peacock blue like an aquarium; outside, the sea is turbulent and dark. When Jack leads Ralph away from the lagoon to the far side of the island, Ralph realizes how the coral reef has protected them from the Pacific. Just as he now begins to see the dark forces in Jack's nature, so he sees the ocean as an enemy.

> Now he saw the landsman's view of the swell and it seemed like the breathing of some stupendous creature. Slowly the waters sank among the rocks, revealing pink tables of granite, strange growths of coral, polyp, and weed. Down, down, the waters went, whispering like the wind among the heads of the forest. There was one flat rock there, spread like a table, and the waters sucking down on the four weedy sides made them seem like cliffs. Then the sleeping leviathan breathed out—the waters rose, the weed streamed, and the water boiled over the table rock with a roar. There was no sense of the passage of waves; only this minute-long fall and rise and fall.

On the other side of the island where the fall into the heart of darkness will begin and Jack will set up his bloody hunters' society above the red cliffs of Castle Rock, the sea becomes an enemy and a threat, a beast and a boundary, preventing all escape.

> The filmy enchantments of mirage could not endure the cold ocean water and the horizon was hard, clipped blue. Ralph wandered down to the rocks. Down here, almost on a level with the sea, you could follow with your eye the ceaseless bulging passage of the deep sea waves. They were miles wide, apparently not breakers or the banked ridges of shallow water. They travelled the length of the island with an air of disregarding it and being set on other business; they were less a progress than a momentous rise and fall of the whole ocean. Now the sea would suck down, making cascades and waterfalls of retreating water, would sink past the rocks and plaster down the seaweed like shining hair; then, pausing, gather and rise with a roar, irresistibly swelling over point and outcrop, climbing the little cliff, sending at last an arm of surf up a gully to end a yard or so from him in fingers of spray.
>
> Wave after wave, Ralph followed the rise and fall until something of the remoteness of the sea numbed his brain. Then gradually the almost infinite size of this water forced itself on his attention. This was the divider, the barrier. On the other side of the island, swathed at midday with mirage, defended by the shield of the quiet lagoon, one might dream of rescue; but here, faced by the brute obtuseness of the ocean, the miles of division, one was clamped down, one was helpless, one was condemned, one was—

There the hunters will live, surrounded by the rise and fall of the great leviathan. There they will sing their bloody chants, "Kill the beast! Cut his throat! Spill his blood!" The encompassing ocean is the beast now, forcing the boys to savagery in order to survive, isolating them from any control of adult society. They are acting out the night terror of the littlun Percival, who imagines the Beast coming up out of the dark sea. It is his terror that first breaks up the boys' meeting and sanity itself. To Ralph, fear and talk of the sea beast is the beginning of chaos. Worse is Jack's breaking of the rules symbolized by the possession of the seashell, the conch, for the rules are the only things they have for survival just as captain's orders are the only things that make a ship survive. After the meeting has dissolved, Ralph confesses, "We're all drifting and things are going rotten. At home there was always a grown-up. Please, sir: please, miss; and then you got an answer. How I wish!" What he wishes is that nobody had believed in a beast from the sea where no beasts are, whence rescue and men's authority always will be.

—Andrew Sinclair, "William Golding's the Sea, the Sea," *Twentieth Century Literature* 28, No. 2 (Summer 1982): 172–74

Kathleen Woodward on Children and Violence

[Kathleen Woodward, a professor of English at the University of Wisconsin at Milwaukee, is the coeditor of *The Technological Imagination* (1980). In this extract, Woodward finds that one of the most important themes in *Lord of the Flies* is its searing depiction of the violence of which children are capable.]

As a fable *Lord of the Flies* may be about the evil in the human heart, but as a novel it is about the frightening potential of children for violence. This is one of the complicated and fascinating effects of the book. The adult world may indeed be marked by extreme brutality—we remember intermittently that an atomic war is in process—but it seems for the moment infinitely preferable to the violent anarchy of children. For in the course of the narrative our suspension of disbelief is so perfectly manipulated by Golding that we temporarily forget that these characters are in fact children and respond to them as if they were adults. Thus, when they are rescued by a naval officer at the end of the story, and we recognize with a shock that they are children after all, we are willing to accept anything but this, even an atomic war, which now seems less savage than the violent obsessions of young Jack and his followers.

True, the conclusion of *Lord of the Flies* is ironic, a kind of frame which sets the fable in place. As Golding asks elsewhere, commenting on the ending of the story, "The officer, having interrupted a manhunt, prepares to take the children off the island in a cruiser which will presently be hunting its enemy in the same implacable way. And who will rescue the adult and his cruiser?" But this is not the only effect of the ending. We welcome with uncomplicated relief the figure of authority. We conclude that children require strict supervision and constant discipline, for without these, they pose a serious threat to the adult world.

Doris Lessing has written about this in her fine novel *Memoirs of a Survivor* (1975), which is also set in a future post-war period. As the narrator, who is an adult, admits, "At the sight of children, I was afraid. And I realized 'in a flash'—another one!—that I, that everybody had come to see all children as, simply, terrifying." The children form angry survival bands. How can they be dealt with? One character concludes that "the only way to cope with the 'kids' was to separate them and put them into households in ones and twos." This is how to deal with the enemy—divide and conquer. In Golding's most recent novel, *Darkness Visible,* which is as sophisticated and phantasmagorical as *Lord of the Flies* is not, children also manifest this capacity for perverse behavior. The young Sophy, a beautiful child much admired for her angelic charm, reflects malevolently about killing her twin sister, whom she thinks receives more attention than she does. Both sisters grow up to be terrorists who not only fantasize about the politics of violence, but practice it. All of this resonates with our contemporary experience. In the newspapers we read of children not yet ten who beat up the elderly, of young babysitters who torture their charges in microwave ovens, of children who try to kill their parents, as the following newspaper clipping about an incident in Slidell, Louisiana, shows:

> Two girls discussed ways of killing their sleeping parents after a family argument, then set fire to their trailer home, police say.
>
> The parents were in a suburban New Orleans hospital Sunday with severe burns over 45% of their bodies.
>
> "They discussed shooting, stabbing, cutting their heads off and finally decided on fire," a sheriff's spokesman said.
>
> Deputies said the murder was planned after the girls, aged 9 and 13, got into an argument with their parents Friday.
>
> The girls were booked with aggravated arson and the attempted murders of Truett Simpson, 51, and his wife, Glenda, 42, who were rescued from their burning mobile home about 3 A.M. Saturday. It was first thought that the daughters died in the fire, but they were found later in New Orleans.

This is evil, an action, like Jack's, so reprehensible that we cannot imagine a punishment for it. As our society grows more severely age-segregated, the generations come to regard each other as alien—the elderly are strangers to the middle-aged, children perceive their parents as belonging to another species, parents are threatened by their children. Much of the power of reading Golding's novel today rests here: the fear of the child as a violent other, virulent in itself, not a mere analogy for adult brutality (which we know better and accept more easily), but a potential enemy who turns, perversely, the screw.

—Kathleen Woodward, "On Aggression: William Golding's *Lord of the Flies*," *No Place Else: Explorations in Utopian and Dystopian Fiction*, ed. Eric S. Rabkin, Martin H. Greenberg, and Joseph D. Olander (Carbondale: Southern Illinois University Press, 1983), pp. 219–20

Philip Redpath on Ralph and Jack

[Philip Redpath, a British literary critic, is the author of *William Golding: A Structural Reading of His Fiction* (1986), from which the following extract is taken. Here, Redpath believes that the figures of Ralph and Jack, who seem to represent the forces of civilization, in fact reveal the failure of civilization in coming to terms with evil.]

What we have with Ralph is not the development of a heroic insight but a study in failure. He fails when he tries to act reasonably against the hunters because he thinks that adults would act reasonably. But civilization denies the darkness of its heart. It covers it with a veneer of reason and then goes out into the world and fights wars; it acts in the same way as Jack and the hunters, except that it is far, far more destructive. Ralph tries to hide the beast in himself by a worship of the adult world. And yet, if at the end Jack and his painted tribe armed with sharpened sticks reflect the well-armed and uniformed officer and his men, Ralph's advocacy of rational behaviour has been nothing but a misplaced advocacy of an illusion or miscomprehension. He has worshipped the lie behind which man attempts to conceal his true nature. Ralph himself displays the rending of this lie when he finds himself longing to hurt Robert—'The desire to squeeze and hurt was over-mastering'—and when at the end of the novel he has become a very efficient savage. Reasonable naval officer and unreasonable savage are reflections of each other. Ralph's failure is that he does not understand this until the end, and Piggy remains obliviously ignorant of it. We can see that James Gindin has missed the point when he asks, 'If the adult world rescues the boys . . . are the depravity and the brutality of human nature so complete?' Ralph and the officer are not in opposition to the savages; there is no difference between them.

We have shared Ralph's perspective for most of the novel and sympathize with him. The change in point of view to the officer is not just to reveal the officer's lack of insight; it is designed to shock us out of our rationalistic complacency by revealing that *Lord of the Flies* is condemning the point of view it has made us read from. Ralph extols the adult world: his father is ironically a naval officer. But the adult world and the savages are no different from each other except in so far as one lies to itself, denies its unreason, and claims to be civilized. Ralph represents the perspective that would conceal the true nature of man and would rationalize acts of inhumanity. At least Jack is honest: ' "We're strong—we hunt! If there's a beast, we'll hunt it down! We'll close in and beat and beat and beat—!" ' Ralph is nearly killed because of his faith in the appearance of reason which is useless when contrasted to man's true nature. His rescue is not a rescue at all if it marks a return to a reflection of the society that has tried to kill him on the island. It must represent some kind of a defeat for him in view of what he at last recognizes about the nature of all men.

—Philip Redpath, *William Golding: A Structural Reading of His Fiction* (London: Vision Press, 1986), pp. 89–90

S. J. BOYD ON CLASS CONSCIOUSNESS IN *LORD OF THE FLIES*

[S. J. Boyd, a lecturer in English at the University of St. Andrews in Scotland, is the author of *The Novels of William Golding* (1988), from which the following extract is taken. Here, Boyd sees one of the chief messages of *Lord of the Flies* to be a condemnation of class divisions in society.]

Golding's later novels, especially *The Pyramid* and *Rites of Passage,* make abundantly clear his deep bitterness at and hatred of the evils of class. But even in this first novel, even on a desert island, this Golding obsession is in evidence. The novelist Ian McEwan has written of his adolescent reading of *Lord of the Flies:* 'As far as I was concerned, Golding's island was a thinly disguised boarding school.' At one point the narrator seems to claim that class is of no importance in the alienation and persecution of Piggy: 'There had grown up tacitly among the biguns the opinion that Piggy was an outsider, not only by accent, which did not matter, but by fat, and ass-mar, and specs, and a certain disinclination for manual labour.' But the narrator implicitly admits that accent, a mark of class, *is* an alienating factor ['not only'] and actually mocks, in passing, Piggy's way of speaking. The view that class does not matter in Piggy's misfortunes is scarcely borne out by events. From the very outset Piggy is isolated, stranded on an island within the island, by being lower-class. On the book's first page Ralph's 'automatic gesture' of pulling up his socks makes 'the jungle seem for a moment like the Home Counties' and unfortunately Piggy just does not fit into the middle-class ambience implied thereby. Ralph is a good-natured boy, but in this initial scene he seems very reluctant to accept the friendship of the one companion he has so far found on the desert island: ' "What's your name?" "Ralph." The fat boy waited to be asked his name in turn but this proffer of acquaintance was not made.' One has the uncomfortable feeling throughout this scene that Ralph has been conditioned to be unfriendly towards boys who talk like Piggy. Ralph is not slow to inform Piggy that his father is officer-class, but in response to the crucial question ' "What's your father?" 'Piggy can produce only the poignant reply: " 'My dad's dead," he said quickly, "and my mum—" ' The unseemly haste with which Piggy announces that his father is dead suggests a reluctance to reveal his place in life and the blank after the mention of his mum speaks unhappy volumes. Piggy has failed to produce satisfactory credentials. It is at least partly for this reason that Piggy is doomed to become 'the centre of social derision so that everyone felt cheerful and normal.' Life seems cheery and normal provided there are the likes of Piggy around to be looked down on and derided.

Piggy's main persecutor is Jack, who from the first evinces contempt and hatred for Piggy, whom he seems to regard as an upstart. Jack's education appears to have instilled in him the belief that it is his right to give commands, to rule: '"I ought to be chief," said Jack with simple arrogance, "because I'm chapter chorister and head boy."' His privileged choir-school background has no doubt taught him much about the necessity of hierarchies, including the notion that head boy from such a school ought to be top man anywhere. ⟨John S.⟩ Whitley comments: 'This assumption of leadership, bred by being part of a civilised élite, is maintained when he becomes a member of a primitive élite. The perfect prefect becomes the perfect savage.' It would be difficult to imagine anything more suggestive of innocence than a group of cathedral choristers, but we first see the choir as 'something dark' in the haze, as 'the darkness': the choir is from the outset associated with evil. A cathedral choir connotes also a certain English middle-class cosiness, a social world 'assured of certain certainties'. Here is Jack at his most 'sensible', declaring some important certainties: '". . . We've got to have rules and obey them. After all, we're not savages. We're English; and the English are best at everything."' Golding has written that such cosy English chauvinism was something he particularly wished to attack in *Lord of the Flies:*

> One of our faults is to believe that evil is somewhere else and inherent in another nation. My book was to say: you think that now the war is over and an evil thing destroyed, you are safe because you are naturally kind and decent.
>
> —S. J. Boyd, *The Novels of William Golding* (Brighton, UK: Harvester Press, 1988), pp. 10–12

✤

L. L. DICKSON ON THE BATTLE MOTIF IN *LORD OF THE FLIES*

[L. L. Dickson, a professor of language and literature at Northern Kentucky University, is the author of *The Modern Allegories of William Golding* (1990), from which the following extract is taken. Here, Dickson studies the battle motif in *Lord of the Flies,* tracing its allegorical significance.]

The battle motif is developed in both physical confrontations and rhetorical "combat." Initially, the pig hunts are ritualized tests of strength and manhood, but when the hunters eventually seek human prey (Simon, Piggy, and finally Ralph) the conflict is between the savage and the civilized; blind emotion and prudent rationality; inhumanity and humanity; evil and good. This conflict is further established in the chapter entitled "The Shell and the Glasses," when Jack's hunters attack Ralph's boys and steal Piggy's glasses. Jack carries the broken spectacles—which have become symbolic of intellect, rationality, and civilization—as ritual proof of his manhood and his power over his enemies: "He was a chief now in truth; and he made stabbing motions with his spear." In the "Castle Rock" chapter, Ralph opposes Jack in what is called a "crisis" situation: "They met with a jolt and bounced apart. Jack swung with his fist at Ralph and caught him on the ear. Ralph hit Jack in the stomach and made him grunt. Then they were facing each other again, panting and furious, but unnerved by each other's ferocity. They became aware of the noise that was the background to this fight, the steady shrill cheering of the tribe behind them."

More subtle forms of "battle"—debate and dialogue—are dramatized in the verbal exchanges between Jack and Ralph. Golding emphasizes their polarity: "They walked along, two continents of experience and feeling, unable to communicate." Later when Jack paints his face and flaunts his bloodied knife, the conflict is heightened: "The two boys faced each other. There was the brilliant world of hunting, tactics, fierce exhilaration, skill; and there was the world of longing and baffled commonsense." When Ralph does not move, Jack and the others have to build their fire in a less ideal place: "By the time the pile [of firewood] was built, they were on different sides of a high barrier." Different sides of the wood, different continents, different worlds—all these scenes intensify the symbolic as well as physical conflict. Here we encounter "a structural principle that becomes Golding's hallmark: a polarity expressed in terms of a moral tension. Thus, there is the rational (the fire-watchers) pitted against the irrational (the hunters)."

In both chapter 2, "Beast from Water," and chapter 8, "Gift for the Darkness," the exchange of views about whether there is a beast or not "becomes a blatant allegory in which each spokesman caricatures the position he defends." Ralph and Piggy think that rules and organization can cure social ills, and that if things "break up," it is because individuals are not remembering that life "is scientific," rational, logical. Jack hates rules, only wishes to hunt, and believes that evil is a mystical, living power that can be appeased by ritual sacrifice. Simon feels that evil is not outside but rather within all human beings, though he is "inarticulate in his effort to express mankind's essential illness." He uses comparisons with excrement and filth to describe his notion of human inner evil.

Simon's confrontation with the pig's head on a stick, the Lord of the Flies, is another instance of allegorical dialogue. At first, Beelzebub seems to triumph: Simon is mesmerized by the grinning face; he is warned that he is "not wanted," for Simon is the only boy who possesses a true vision of the nature of evil; and finally he faints. However, Simon recovers, asks himself, "What else is there to do?," discovers the dead parachutist, and then takes the news about the "beast" to the rest of the boys. The entire scene with the pig's head represents the conflict that is occurring within Simon's own consciousness. The Lord of the Flies is only an externalization of the inner evil in all humans. Later when Ralph comes upon the pig's head, "the skull [stares at] Ralph like one who knows all the answers and won't tell." Though Ralph does not understand the significance of the pig, he does feel a "sick fear." In desperation he hits the head, as if breaking it would destroy the evil on the island. However, the broken pig's head lies in two pieces, "its grin now six feet across." Rather than being destroyed, it ironically has grown. In the final pages of the novel, when Ralph is desperately fleeing from the hunters, he runs in circles and retraces his steps back to the broken pig's head, and this time its "fathom-wide grin" entirely dominates the burning island.

—L. L. Dickson, *The Modern Allegories of William Golding* (Tampa: University of South Florida Press, 1990), pp. 18–19

PATRICK REILLY ON *LORD OF THE FLIES* AND *GULLIVER'S TRAVELS*

[Patrick Reilly is the author of *Jonathan Swift: The Brave Desponder* (1982), *George Orwell: The Age's Adversity* (1986), and *The Literature of Guilt: From Gulliver to Golding* (1987). In this extract from Reilly's book on *Lord of the Flies,* Reilly studies the many parallels it holds to Jonathan Swift's *Gulliver's Travels.*]

What is still to be adequately recognized is the extent to which *Lord of the Flies* replicates the ground plan of *Gulliver's Travels,* unearthing the same discoveries, climaxing in an analogous impasse. Both texts compel us to scrutinize anew those slothful assumptions we so carelessly take for knowledge. Who are the savages in Gulliver's last voyage—those who try to kill him with poisoned arrows or those in Portugal who, if they heard his story would burn him in the fires of the Inquisition? Officially, the former are savages, the latter civilized. Swift asks if we are happy with this demarcation. In *Lord of the Flies* Golding shows us a boy with a stick and a man with a nuclear warship and asks us to say which is the greater threat to life. Yet we still have so much irrelevant labor expended on arguments as to whether *Lord of the Flies* is a "tory" text, an implicit tribute to the salutary disciplines of society, bereft of which, men must lapse into ruinous anarchy. To see Golding as the heir of Swift would prevent such misguided industry, for no more than his master does Golding promise salvation in the city or declare that only in the jungle are we at risk. Nature is as much a metaphor in Golding as in Bunyan. When Ralph laments "the wearisomeness of this life, where every path was an improvisation and a considerable part of one's waking life was spent watching one's feet," his immediate reference is, of course, to the literal difficulty of walking in the jungle, but the wider, metaphorical implications are unmistakable. It would be as foolish to believe that fear and frustration are confined to the tropics as to take the Slough of Despond for a criticism of the local roads authority. As much as Swift, Golding denies the segregation of jungle and home countries; the problems are the same, merely transposed to a new setting and wearing a different vestment. That is the meaning of that concluding parallax when the rescuing officer arrives and the perspective is so startlingly altered. Here, too, Gulliver's legacy is evident, for Swift reveals himself in Lilliput and Brobdingnag as the master of perspective, and Golding proves an exemplary pupil in his own virtuoso performance throughout his book.

The parallels multiply on inspection. Islands are ideal for such fictions, providing the perfect laboratory conditions—hermetic, remote, fenced off from irrelevance—for the testing of human nature. Gulliver protests the irrelevance of his writings to affairs at home: how could events so distant be applicable to the state of England? Golding's adventure story has a parallel deceptiveness. What have the actions of a bunch of boys stranded on an island to do with us, except to provide a pleasant way of passing our time? Yet Golding as much as Gulliver writes for our amendment, not our entertainment. These travels abroad disclose the truth of home. Gulliver is soon indignantly demanding how any reader dare question the authenticity of the Yahoos when they abound in London and Dublin—admittedly wearing clothes and using a jabber of language, but undeniably Yahoos for all that. One recalls how American publishers initially rejected *Animal Farm* on the ground that there was no market for animal stories. *Lord of the Flies* is a boys' adventure story in the sense that *Animal Farm* is an animal story or *Gulliver's Travels* a piece of travel literature. Behind the facade of all three is a warning and an exhortation: attention must be paid, for it is a matter of salvation. *Lord of the Flies* is only ostensibly about the rescue of Ralph; much more pertinent and taxing is the problem of the rescuer's rescue, the salvation of the savior. This is the real problem of the text, insoluble within its pages, pressing upon the book's readers: here the author makes no claim to authority. In this challenge to the reader (audible, surely, even without the prompting of Golding's extratextual tuition), the text links up with contemporary works like *The Fall* and *Nineteen Eighty-four,* all manifestly derivative of *Gulliver's Travels.* Is it necessary to repeat that to use "derivative" in such a context is the highest compliment that one can pay?

—Patrick Reilly, Lord of the Flies: *Fathers and Sons* (New York: Twayne, 1992), pp. 40–41

✤

Works by William Golding

Poems. 1934.

Lord of the Flies. 1954.

The Inheritors. 1955.

Pincher Martin. 1956.

The Brass Butterfly. 1958.

Free Fall. 1959.

The Spire. 1964.

The Hot Gates and Other Occasional Pieces. 1965.

The Pyramid. 1967.

Talk: Conversations with William Golding (with Jack I. Biles). 1970.

The Scorpion God: Three Short Novels. 1971.

Darkness Visible. 1979.

Rites of Passage. 1980.

A Moving Target. 1982.

Nobel Lecture: 7 December 1983. 1984.

The Paper Men. 1984.

Lord of the Flies; Pincher Martin; Rites of Passage. 1984.

An Egyptian Journal. 1985.

Close Quarters. 1987.

Fire Down Below. 1989.

To the Ends of the Earth: A Sea Trilogy 〈*Rites of Passage, Close Quarters, Fire Down Below*〉. 1991.

The Double Tongue: A Draft of a Novel. 1995.

Works about William Golding and *Lord of the Flies*

Baker, James R. "The Decline of *Lord of the Flies.*" *South Atlantic Quarterly* 69 (1970): 446–60.

———. *William Golding: A Critical Study.* New York: St. Martin's Press, 1965.

———, ed. *Critical Essays on William Golding.* Boston: G. K. Hall, 1988.

Biles, Jack I., and Robert O. Evans, ed. *William Golding: Some Critical Considerations.* Lexington: University Press of Kentucky, 1978.

Bufkin, E. C. "*Lord of the Flies:* An Analysis." *Georgia Review* 19 (1965): 40–57.

Capey, A. C. "Will and Idea in *Lord of the Flies.*" *Use of English* 24 (1972–73): 99–107.

Carey, John. *William Golding: The Man and His Books: A Tribute on His 75th Birthday.* New York: Farrar, Straus & Giroux, 1987.

Clark, George. "An Illiberal Education: William Golding's Pedagogy." In *Seven Contemporary Authors,* ed. Thomas B. Whitbread. Austin: University of Texas Press, 1966, pp. 73–95.

Cox, C. B. "*Lord of the Flies.*" *Critical Quarterly* 2 (1960): 112–17.

Crompton, Dan. *A View from the Spire: William Golding's Later Novels.* Completed by Julia Briggs. Oxford: Basil Blackwell, 1985.

Dicken-Fuller, Nicola C. *William Golding's Use of Symbolism.* Lewes, UK: Book Guild, 1990.

Elman, Paul. *William Golding: A Critical Study.* Grand Rapids, MI: Eerdmans, 1967.

Fitzgerald, John F., and John R. Kayser. "Golding's *Lord of the Flies:* Pride as Original Sin." *Studies in the Novel* 24 (1992): 78–88.

Fleck, A. D. "The Golding Bough: Aspects of Myth and Ritual in *Lord of the Flies.*" In *On the Novel,* ed. B. S. Benedikz. London: Dent, 1971, pp. 189–205.

Friedman, Lawrence S. *William Golding.* New York: Continuum, 1993.

Gekoski, R. A., and P. A. Grogan. *William Golding: A Bibliography 1934–1993.* London: Andre Deutsch, 1994.

Gindin, James. *William Golding.* New York: St. Martin's Press, 1988.

Granofsky, Ronald. " 'Man at an Extremity': Elemental Trauma and Revelation in the Fiction of William Golding." *Modern Language Studies* 20 (1990): 50–63.

Hadomi, Leah. "Imagery as a Source of Irony in Golding's *Lord of the Flies.*" *Hebrew University Studies in Literature and the Arts* 9 (1981): 126–38.

Hodson, Leighton. *William Golding.* Edinburgh: Oliver & Boyd, 1969.

Hynes, Samuel. *William Golding.* New York: Columbia University Press, 1964.

Johnston, Arnold. *Of Earth and Darkness: The Novels of William Golding.* Columbia: University of Missouri Press, 1980.

Josipovici, Gabriel. "Golding: The Hidden Source." In Josipovici's *The World and the Book: A Study of Modern Fiction.* London: Macmillan, 1971, pp. 236–55.

Kermode, Frank. "The Novels of William Golding." *International Literary Annual* 1 (1961): 11–29.

MacShane, Frank. "The Novels of William Golding." *Dalhousie Review* 42 (1962–63): 171–83.

Martin, Jerome. "Symbol Hunting in Golding's *Lord of the Flies.*" *English Journal* 58 (1969): 45–56.

Medcalf, Stephen. *William Golding.* Harlow, UK: British Council/Longmans, 1975.

Mitchell, Charles. "*Lord of the Flies* and the Escape from Freedom." *Arizona Quarterly* 22 (1966): 27–40.

O'Hara, J. D. "Mute Choirboys and Angelic Pigs: The Fable in *Lord of the Flies.*" *Texas Studies in Literature and Language* 7 (1965–66): 411–20.

Pemberton, Clive. *William Golding*. Harlow, UK: British Council & National Book League/Longmans, 1969.

Peter, John. "The Fables of William Golding." *Kenyon Review* 19 (1957): 577–92.

Rexroth, Kenneth. "William Golding." *Atlantic Monthly* 215, No. 5 (May 1965): 96–98.

Rosenberg, Bruce A. "Lord of the Fire-flies." *Centennial Review* 11 (1967): 128–39.

Rosenfield, Claire. "Men of a Smaller Growth: A Psychological Analysis of William Golding's *Lord of the Flies.*" *Literature and Psychology* 11 (1961): 93–96.

Spitz, David. "Power and Authority: An Interpretation of Golding's *Lord of the Flies.*" *Antioch Review* 30 (1970–71): 21–33.

Stinson, John J. "Trying to Exorcise the Beast: The Grotesque in the Fiction of William Golding." *Cithara* 11 (1971): 3–30.

Talon, Henri. "Irony in *Lord of the Flies.*" *Essays in Criticism* 18 (1968): 296–309.

Tiger, Virginia. *William Golding: The Dark Fields of Discovery.* London: Calder & Boyars, 1974.

Townsend, R. C. "*Lord of the Flies:* Fool's Gold?" *Journal of General Education* 16 (1964): 153–60.

Twentieth Century Literature 28, No. 2 (Summer 1982). Special William Golding issue.

Whitley, John S. *Golding:* Lord of the Flies. London: Edward Arnold, 1970.

Index of Themes and Ideas